STRANGLER'S MOON

A silent killer using the ancient methods of the stranglers of India; an unknown traitor; and an alluring but ruthless Indian beauty: these were some of the enemies ranged against Paul Mason when he answered a plea for help from an old friend. In Kashmir, Mason is soon engulfed in violence and intrigue. Events lead to the Himalayan plateau on the borders of China and Tibet, where he relentlessly pursues his enemies to a final challenge . . .

CHARLES LEADER

STRANGLER'S MOON

Complete and Unabridged

LINFORD
Leicester

First published in Great Britain

First Linford Edition
published 1998

Copyright © 1968 by Charles Leader
All rights reserved

British Library CIP Data

Leader, Charles, *1938–*
Strangler's moon.—Large print ed.—
Linford mystery library
1. Detective and mystery stories
2. Large type books
I. Title
823.9'14 [F]

ISBN 0–7089–5224–0

Published by
F. A. Thorpe (Publishing) Ltd.
Anstey, Leicestershire

Set by Words & Graphics Ltd.
Anstey, Leicestershire
Printed and bound in Great Britain by
T. J. International Ltd., Padstow, Cornwall

This book is printed on acid-free paper

1

The Kiss of Khali

The sentry knew nothing of his own death. There was just the silent movement of a shadow in the moonlight, something that might have been a black bird flashing swiftly past his face, and then the abrupt snapping of his neck. His head was jerked sharply backwards and to the right, and his mouth was half open with the tongue just beginning to protrude. His body stiffened and balanced grotesquely on its heels, and then his hands opened to let the sub-machine-gun slip from his fingers and fall on to the damp grass at his feet. The soft earth muffled the sound, and as the sentry's body fell backwards it was supported by his murderer who lowered him almost tenderly to the ground.

The night air was cool, and the pale face of the moon merged back into the dark curtains of cloud as though shocked

1

by what it had seen. The army camp sprawled silent and undisturbed at the foot of the thousand-foot hill, and in the distance the great ice peaks of the Himalayas were hidden by the night. All was still and there was no sign that the removal of the sentry had been noticed. He had been patrolling alone along the perimeter of the camp, and now nothing moved except the soft breeze that bore the faint golden-leaved scents of autumn along the Kashmir valley.

The murderer listened, was satisfied, and then knelt by the body of his victim. With deft fingers he freed the strangling scarf from the sentry's throat, and drew the filmy black silk lovingly through his fingers until he encountered the coin which weighted the end. His lips shaped a smile without showing his teeth and his heart was beating with faint exhilaration. His face was thin and brown, and hollowed out around the bones. His eyes were deeply sunken, and in the exact centre of his forehead was painted the vertical mark which indicated a follower of Shiva The Destroyer.

The man arose, ignored the fallen sub-machine-gun, and began to run swiftly towards the outline of the nearest block of barrack buildings. He reached them without creating any alarm and melted into the blackness against the nearest wall. His bare feet made no sound, either on the grass or the concrete paths that threaded through the barracks, and he was dressed in black cotton trousers and a black shirt which enabled him to blend unseen into the night. He picked his way unerringly through the long huts of sleeping soldiers, avoiding any further sentries, and at last halting by the administrative buildings of the Command Headquarters.

He wrinkled his brows, trying to remember all that he had been told, and then circled cautiously round to the back of the block. The scrape of boots on the concrete path warned him not to turn the second corner and he crouched low in a patch of total shadow. His fingers touched the silk scarf, but there were two men approaching and so he became still. Two military policemen passed, burly

Sikhs on a routine patrol. The moon was still lurking behind the clouds, as though reluctant to witness any further violence, and so the two Sikhs continued their measured tread without noticing the intruder. When they had disappeared the man turned the corner and ran along the back of the building.

He passed several closed windows until he found the one he sought, a small window that was partially open as he had been told it would be. The top half of the window opened outwards and upwards. He pushed it up and then heaved himself up to wriggle his head and shoulders through the opening. The smell struck into his nostrils but did not unduly bother him. He had expected the smell. That was why the window was habitually left open. The window frame was a tight fit, and he had to twist his thin body to one side in order to squeeze his shoulders through. He got one arm free and groped along the inner wall to his left until he found a firm grip on the main water pipe of the lavatory cistern and then he was able to haul himself inside. For a moment he clung like an agile monkey to the cistern tank, and then he lowered himself carefully. The toilet was the squatting type and he kept his back against the wall to avoid stepping into the hole. The chain rattled against the wall as he brushed past it to the door and his heart gave a skittering jump. It was the first sound that he had made.

He stepped out into the corridor and closed the door behind him. The darkness was absolute and from his trouser pocket he drew a small, hooded torch that was restricted to a narrow pencil beam. He used it to find his way along the corridor until he came to a T junction where he turned left. He counted the doors on his right and at the fourth door he stopped. The door was locked but from his pocket the intruder drew a large bunch of keys. His fingers were nervous now as he fitted them one by one into the lock, but with the seventh key the lock turned. The silent intruder entered quickly and closed the door behind him.

There was a large square of lesser darkness which marked the only window in the room and he crossed towards it. He switched off his torch for a moment and peered through the glass, but there was nothing outside to disturb him. Reassured he switched the torch on again and used the tiny beam to examine the room. He was in an office that was coldly furnished with a large desk table and two spartan chairs. Opposite the window the whole wall was covered with military maps of the area and of India as a whole. Behind the desk were solid ranks of grey-painted steel filing cabinets, and above those were framed portraits of Gandhi and Nehru.

The intruder was interested only in the filing cabinets and specifically in two drawers. He had to think a moment to remember which these were, and his lips moved in a faint mutter as he counted the horizontal and vertical lines of the drawers. When he had selected the right two he again produced his bunch of skeleton keys and tried the smaller ones in the locks. One drawer he opened but the second resisted all his efforts. He began to bite his lip for now he had to make a little noise, and then he took a heavy screwdriver from his belt. He went to the window and checked that there were no sentries in sight, and then started on the task of forcing the lock.

It took him nearly fifteen minutes to break the drawer open, and by that time his nerves were signalling the first alarm warnings of panic. He knew that if he delayed too long the dead sentry would be found and the alarm raised before he could escape. The lock gave with a harsh, tearing sound that rendered him immobile in the darkness. He listened tensely and then checked the window again before he came back to the files. He turned over the stiff brown folders with thin, bony fingers and selected the ones he needed from each drawer. They all bore the special security stamp which he had been told to look for. He took these folders over to the desk and then dug into his pocket for the small micro-camera and began to take photographs of each typewritten page.

The camera had been pre-set and he had been instructed carefully on how to use it. The whole job took him just over

7

five minutes and afterwards he returned the folders and closed the drawers of the filing cabinet. His camera now contained a microfilmed record of the full Indian military strength in the disputed areas of Kashmir and Ladakh; complete lists of tanks, arms and troops, and their positions of deployment, whether facing China or Pakistan. The intruder did not know this, but was simply following instructions.

There was one final instruction to be followed and he almost forgot. He left the office and was about to relock the door behind him when he remembered. He hesitated and then returned to the filing cabinet. From his pocket he took a handwritten page of folded notepaper and allowed it to flutter to the floor. The job was done and he left hurriedly.

He retraced his steps and made his exit through the toilet window, emerging head first and slithering clumsily down the wall to the ground. Outside the moon was still sulking behind the clouds, and that was a good sign. The dark confines of the building had unnerved him, but

8

his confidence returned now that he was back in the open. He followed his route of entry, moving fast and keeping to the shadows as he doubled back through the lanes between the barrack blocks. He reached the last block and then froze against the corner of the building as the moon suddenly chose to drift out into a gap between the clouds. In the same moment he realized that there was another sentry standing less than six yards away.

The soldier had his back turned and appeared to be waiting for something or someone. His sub-machine-gun was slung by its strap across his shoulder and he was looking out towards the perimeter of the camp. The intruder stared at the broad back and suddenly sensed the truth. The sentry was waiting for his comrade who had been killed. Perhaps the two were in the habit of meeting for a sly smoke, or at least of exchanging an acknowledgment as the path of their patrols crossed. Either way the second sentry had become suspicious, and it was only a matter of moments before he would start to investigate and ultimately find the body.

The intruder sucked a silent breath through his teeth, and then his hands moved to his waist and gently tugged free the silk scarf that was tucked into his trousers. He tightened his grip, and then stepped round the corner of the building and struck.

The weighted scarf gave a feathery hiss as it unfolded through the air. It curled around the sentry's neck with a vicious bite and the intruder jerked with a quick snap of his wrist to break the unsuspecting man's neck. Again he caught the body and lowered it down on to the damp grass.

He stared down at his second victim and this time the elation coursed more strongly through his veins. Each man had tasted the silken kiss of Khali, and the black scarf was proving a more silent and effective weapon than even he had believed possible. He understood now how the stranglers of the early nineteenth century had terrorized the whole of India with this simple method of killing, and he wondered if he too should pray to Khali, the female manifestation of the Destroyer-God Shiva whose mark was branded on his forehead. The stranglers had been devotees of the cult of Khali, and when using their methods perhaps it would be wise to offer prayers to the Goddess.

It was an ethical question he would consider later. In the meantime he retrieved his scarf and ran swiftly across the open space to the edge of the camp. He passed the stiffening body of the first sentry he had killed and then scrambled up and over the high, encircling fence. There was no outcry, and no alarm. He dropped down on the far side and vanished into the night.

2

A Call for Help

Paul Mason stood on the lower deck of the star ferry as it chugged its way slowly across the glittering blue harbour between Kowloon and Hong Kong. Across the bay a large fishing junk under full sail was attracting the attention of a husband and wife tourist couple who were standing on Mason's left, while on his right a small group of American servicemen on leave from Vietnam were fussing hastily with their cameras. Behind him on the packed rows of wooden seats the Chinese passengers treated the scene with placid disregard, while Mason himself stared broodingly into the water.

The crossing took five minutes and Mason was faintly startled when the ferry boat bumped against the far pier. He looked up at the soaring white buildings and then realized that

12

behind him the Chinese were jostling towards the gangway. He turned away from the rail to follow them, and when he straightened up his height was a mere inch below six foot. He held the rank of Captain in the Royal Marines but today he was not in uniform. In fact, it was a long time since he had worn a uniform at all. He was normally alert and brisk but today he was slow and thoughtful. In the general exodus he was pressed up against a young Chinese girl, and his lack of interest made her bold enough to look up at him with curious eyes. His dark, well-cut suit did not hide the fact that he was hard-muscled and physically fit, and she sensed that his serious face would normally be gay. He had clearly seen quite a lot of Asian sunshine, but his hands and face had tanned a healthy brown instead of the blistery red which seemed the fate of so many Englishmen in the east. She liked the deep blue colour of his eyes, but then the crowds parted them and she was too polite to look back. Mason walked on without ever having noticed that she existed.

He emerged on to Connaught Road Central and boarded a bus, squeezing into the only vacant seat. Ten minutes later he dismounted high up the slope of Victoria Peak, and by then he had made his decision, or more exactly he had reinforced the decision which he had made when he had telephoned his chief earlier from his apartment in Kowloon. He straightened his shoulders and walked more smartly the rest of the way, to the headquarters of the Far Eastern division of British Naval Intelligence.

In the large office where the single wide window faced out over the harbour and the Kowloon peninsula on the far side Lieutenant-Commander Allan Kendall was scowling through a typewritten report. He threw it down with relief as Mason was announced and said gloomily, "Young Baxter has definite talent, but not as an Intelligence officer. He'd make a better poet. He makes his report on that sabotage job on the *Vindictive* read like Shakespearian drama."

Mason calculated his superior's mood and decided not to smile. He closed the door behind him and said calmly, "Yes, sir. But at least he does a good job, he's proved a solid case for a court martial."

"That's irrelevant," Kendall snorted. "I expect that. I don't expect flowing prose from official reports."

He leaned back in his chair, a movement which meant that the subject was dismissed, and then invited Mason to sit. He eyed him speculatively and then asked, "What's your problem, Paul?"

Mason smiled. "Not exactly a problem, sir, just a request. Business is slack now that Baxter's nailed that stoker on the *Vindictive*. The horizon seems quiet and I'd like to put in a request for a couple of weeks of back leave."

Kendall frowned and leaned forward once more.

"You've got several weeks due, so I have no real objections. In fact I was thinking of suggesting that you take a break while we can spare you." He paused. "But why so abruptly, Paul? Yesterday there was no indication that

15

you wanted a holiday, yet today you telephone and ask to see me as early as possible the moment I step into the office. What's the rush?"

Mason said, "I expected that. This is the answer." He reached into the inside pocket of his jacket and drew out a folded slip of paper which he passed over the desk. "This cable arrived this morning. It's marked urgent, and I believe it."

Kendall stared at him for a moment, and then he opened out the cable and spread it upon his blotter. He read the three typewritten sentences in a toneless voice.

"Paul. I am in need of help. I will be at the Orient Hotel in New Delhi on the eighth. Please meet me. Panjit Sangh."

Kendall looked up again and his face became sardonic.

"Very dramatic, Paul. And steeped in the tradition of Bulldog Drummond. But what's it all about? And who the hell is Panjit Sangh?"

Mason said quietly, "Do you remember

16

the job I handled in India in sixty-two?[1]
There was a series of raids on our arms
depots here and in Singapore, and some
of the stolen weapons turned up on the
North Eastern frontier when the Red
Chinese started to invade Assam. Panjit
Sangh was the young Lieutenant who was
assigned as my liasion officer with the
Indian Army. He helped me to recover
the stolen rifles."

Kendall nodded. "I remember." He
read through the cable again, and then
asked dubiously, "But it still doesn't
explain what this is all about. New Delhi
is two thousand miles from here, and yet
this fellow Sangh apparently expects you
to drop everything and come running to
his aid, with no clue as to what kind of
trouble he might be in. That's asking a
hell of a lot from a man you haven't
seen for four years, and yet you are
prepared to go. Why, Paul? You're no
schoolboy hero. This kind of thing went

[1] See: Frontier of Violence.

17

out of fashion with gaslight and hansom cabs. It's fifty years out of date and ten thousand miles out of place. It's not your line at all."

Mason drew a long, deep breath, and then tried to explain.

"Sir, it's because Sangh is asking such a hell of a lot that I know he must be in real trouble. And it's not just something that threatens him personally. He's got too much pride to beg help merely on his own account. Sending that cable means that he's facing something desperate. Today is the sixth which gives me just two days, barely enough time to confirm whether or not I can make it. He doesn't even ask me to confirm. The whole thing reads like a grab at a straw. I've considered this as fully as I can in the short time since it arrived, and I'm convinced that something vital is at stake. It has to be something more important than Sangh's pride, and that means more important than his life."

Kendall grimaced, and then asked, "What do you know of Sangh? Is he still in the army?"

"No. He was invalided out in 1963. He was riding in an army jeep that took a nosedive into a ravine somewhere in northern India. His right leg was trapped and they made a mess of getting him out. He spent several months in an army hospital and then they discharged him with a pension and a pair of sticks. He's now living in Srinagar and the last time I heard from him he was trying to make a better living by writing a military history of India."

Kendall glanced down at the cable once more, frowned, and then said slowly, "I had noticed that this originated from Srinagar, but that's several hundred miles from Delhi, and makes me wonder why he has to come south to meet you? And why does he need you at all? If he is in trouble then why is he unable to go to the Indian police? Or his own military authorities? He must surely have contacts from his service days. I'll accept your judgement that if he did in actual fact send this cable then he must be up to his neck in something pretty serious which he can no longer handle, but whatever

19

it is I don't like the idea of you being involved."

He looked up and continued. "Srinagar is the capital of Kashmir. A very beautiful area so they tell me, but also it's a very touchy one politically. There's a conflict of religions between Muslims and Hindus, and only a few months ago it caused India to go to war with Pakistan. For the moment the war is over, but the dust is barely settled and the problem still isn't solved. Also the Chinese are breathing over the northern frontier. They grabbed a big chunk of Ladakh in 63, and they're all set to do it again. That makes three nations with assorted interests and ambitions, and I can imagine the stink that would be aroused by all three if a British Intelligence officer was to be exposed in the area. The usual howls of interference by everyone from the Russians to the Pitcairn Islanders, and a direct rocket to this office in general, and to me in particular for letting you go."

Mason said quietly, "I appreciate that, but Delhi isn't in Kashmir."

"Don't be naïve, Paul. Delhi is only the

first stop. You say that your friend Sangh wouldn't beg help on his own account, and assuming that your judgement is correct then we can further assume that his problem must be nearing a national or international level. We know that he's living in Kashmir and so it's also safe to assume that the problem stems from that area. And furthermore, Sangh knows that you are a British Intelligence officer with experience in most forms of investigation and espionage, which means that it is almost certainly your professional help that he needs."

Mason sat silent for a moment, drumming his fingers reflectively on the top of the desk. He said at last, "I had reasoned that out, sir. In fact, as the last time we worked together was against the Red Chinese it seems reasonable to suppose that the trouble is again threatening from that quarter. He knows that my sympathies and Britain's interests would again be on his side."

Kendall said frankly, "All right, let's assume that he has fallen foul of the Reds. There still remains the question of why he doesn't approach the Indian authorities, or his own Military Intelligence for help? The fact that he wants to meet you outside Kashmir suggests that he's in trouble with his own people. I just don't like the sound of it."

Mason said bluntly, "Sir, I can only be sure of two things. One is that Panjit Sangh is as loyal to India as you are to this department. And two is that he is seriously in need of help. I'll put into writing my request for two weeks back leave."

Kendall looked at him for a moment and then stood up from the desk. He walked across to the window and stood there with his hands folded behind him as he gazed out across the bay. It was a habitual pose that he held for several minutes, and when he answered he did not turn round.

"You can take it as granted, Paul. You have two weeks leave as from tomorrow."

Mason stood up and slowly joined him by the window.

"Thank you, Commander."

They continued to look down upon the

bay for a moment, and then Kendall said, "The last time you were picked up by the Chinese. It could have been damned awkward for me if you hadn't managed to escape. Play it more carefully this time and don't take any risks. Find out what the trouble is, and if you possibly can, persuade your Indian friend to dump his problem on to his own people. And while you're there, bring back a shawl for my wife. She's always wanted a genuine cashmere shawl."

★ ★ ★

Mason was lucky in that he was able to get a free ride in a naval transport plane as far as Singapore, but from there he had to travel at his own expense. He had a four hour wait before he was able to board an Air India jet for New Delhi, and it was mid-day on the eighth when the aircraft landed him at Palam International airport. The sun was blazing from a brassy sky as he walked down the gangway, and the air had a hotter and drier taste than that of Hong Kong.

The passengers walked to the airport buildings and filed through the controls. No visa was necessary for a British national and Mason's passport received only a brief glance as it was stamped. The passport was perfectly in order except that it did not give his true occupation or his military rank. The customs officer decided that he was not the type to smuggle in any illegal rupees, but warned him against changing any sterling on the black market as he handed over the routine currency declaration form. Mason was about to move on when another official checked him.

"Excuse me, sir. Would you tell me please the name of your hotel?"

Mason hesitated, and then told him.

"Ah yes, the Orient Hotel. That is near Connaught Place. May I suggest, sir, that you take a taxi direct to your hotel, and if possible stay there until tomorrow. New Delhi has been subjected to serious riots and the streets are not wholly safe. I must apologize for this inconvenience, but tomorrow it is hoped that things will be back to normal."

Mason stared. "What's the trouble?"

"The Sacred Cow, sir." The official was most apologetic. "In India the cow is held sacred, and the people are protesting against the suggestion that cows should be slaughtered for meat."

Mason grimaced, accepted the warning and passed on. Six separate taxi drivers spotted him as he emerged from the airport and he threw his small suitcase at the eager young Sikh who led the noisy rush towards him. The youth caught the case, shouted off his competitors and then opened the door of his cab for Mason to climb inside. He put the case in the back, slid behind the wheel and pulled off with a last derisive grin at his friends.

During the ride into Delhi Mason asked his driver casual questions about the situation in the city, and the young Sikh gave him voluble and excited details of the riots. Very little sense or reason emerged, however, and at the end of the ride Mason was still unsure whether the man was in favour or against the slaughtering of the Holy Cow. They passed one overturned and burned-out car, and there was plenty of evidence of smashed windows as they entered the swarming city centre, but for the moment the streets seemed quiet. Mason paid off the taxi outside the Orient Hotel, picked up his case and went inside.

He had cabled from Singapore to reserve a room, and found that the room was all ready for him. There were no messages, which puzzled him, but he left instructions that he should be called the moment anyone mentioned his name. An elderly Hindu in a waiter's white coat and trousers showed him to his room, which was modest but spotlessly clean. When the man had gone Mason threw his case on the bed and stripped off his jacket. He was already sweating in the heat and he was tired. He decided to shower and then sleep until the day became cooler.

As he shed his clothes he wondered dubiously what had happened to Panjit Sangh. The young Indian had sounded so urgent in his request for help that Mason had fully expected to find him waiting at the hotel. The rioting was a factor that neither of them could have anticipated and he remembered that Sangh was now hampered by a crippled leg. The Sikh taxi-driver had said that several people had been killed and many injured in the previous day's riots, and Mason hoped that his friend had come to no harm.

He decided then that he was worrying too soon. Sangh would have enough sense to stay clear of the riots, although they had most probably delayed him. Reassured by this reasoning Mason peeled off his socks and walked naked to the shower. He went into the bathroom, pulled back the plastic curtain, and then stopped dead as he stared down into the wide brown eyes of a horrified young Indian girl.

3

Curfew City

Mason tensed, every muscle in his body becoming suddenly alert, and then the scared look in the girl's eyes told him that she offered no threat. Her head barely came up to his shoulder and her hair was drawn back tightly into a long black plait. Her dark brown face was attractive, almost beautiful despite her half startled, half frightened expression. She wore an expensive sari of dark blue silk and he judged her age between twenty-three and twenty-five. His gaze dropped briefly to her hands. They were clasped in front of her and held neither gun nor knife. Mason relaxed and remembered that he was naked.

"Excuse me," he said politely.

He turned away and located a towel which he wrapped calmly around his waist. He tucked in the corner to fasten it in place and then faced his unexpected visitor once more. She still stood in the shower cubicle, but now her eyes were downcast and a faint flush was spreading across her cheeks.

Mason smiled. "I'm sorry about that, but you really shouldn't hide in other people's bathrooms." He paused and added, "You do speak English, I hope?"

The girl raised her head and looked bravely into his face.

"I do speak English, and it is I who should apologize. I — "

Her explanation faltered and Mason took her by the arm and helped her to step out of the shower. "Come into the bedroom," he said. "And then you can tell me who you are, and what you are doing in my bathroom." He gave her an appraising glance and added the warning, "Your sari is far too beautiful to belong to a member of the staff, so don't tell me any untrue stories."

The girl allowed herself to be led out into the bedroom and sat down uncomfortably in the bedside chair. Mason seated himself on the bed, made sure that his towel was respectably fulfilling its function, and then gazed sternly into her hesitant eyes.

"Now," he said. "Who are you?"

"My name is Shareena," she said it simply and without hesitation. "And I am a friend of Panjit Sangh."

Mason's face was blank. "Who is Panjit Sangh?"

She stared at him, and suddenly the brown eyes radiated genuine alarm.

"You mean — you are not Captain Paul Mason?"

Mason gazed deep into her eyes for a moment and then believed her. He smiled gently and said, "I'm sorry. I'm over-cautious. Yes, I am Paul Mason. But tell me about Sangh. Is he here in New Delhi?"

She looked down. "No, that is why I am here in his place. Panjit is still in Srinagar. He is — he is under open arrest by the Military Police."

Mason's face tightened, but it was not wholly unexpected. He reflected grimly that Kendall had been right, and for almost a minute his fingers drummed a slow, silent accompaniment to his thoughts on the taut covers of the bed. At last he said, "You'd better start at the beginning, Shareena. First tell me how and why you came to be hiding in the shower?"

She looked embarrassed, fumbled for a place to start, and then began awkwardly, "Panjit was placed under open arrest yesterday morning, just a few hours before he was to fly from Srinagar to Amritsar, and then to Delhi to meet you. So he asked me to come in his place. I took his seat on the plane, but I was followed. There was an Indian on the plane who was watching me. I could *feel* his eyes upon me. I thought at first that perhaps I was being foolish, that perhaps he just liked to stare at pretty girls, but when we arrived at Delhi I thought it safer not to come direct to this hotel. I went to another hotel on the opposite side of the city, and this man booked a room close to mine in the same hotel. I knew then that he must have followed me from the airport, but what could I do? If I had reported him to the management or the

31

police, he would have simply said that it was a coincidence that we came to the same hotel."

She stopped, as though expecting him to criticize or comment, but Mason merely told her to continue. Her hands fidgeted in her lap but she began again.

"The man made no attempt to speak to me, but in the evening when I came down from my room he was sitting in the hotel lounge. I had to pass through it to go out, and I knew that if I did then he would follow me. I was sure then that he was only watching my movements, to see where I went, and whom I would meet. So I went back to my room. This morning I left very early in order to get out before he was awake. I had breakfast in a restaurant and sat there for perhaps two hours to let the time pass. Then the waiters began to stare at me and I felt I had to leave. I hoped that by then you might have arrived, and so I came here to the Orient Hotel. They told me at the desk that you had booked this room, but would not be arriving until noon, and then I did not know what to do. I could not go back to my own hotel where that man would again begin following me, and it would be unsafe to walk the streets of Delhi. You must know that there have been terrible riots here. Yesterday thousands of Hindus tried to storm the Parliament buildings, and the police had to open fire on the mobs. Five people were killed and many more injured. Today there has been more trouble and the city is under a two-day curfew."

Shareena looked at him helplessly. "I could not go back to my own hotel. I was afraid to go out on to the streets. I have no friends here in Delhi and nowhere else to go. Also I had to see you, to keep my appointment for Panjit Sangh. So I came up here to your room. No one saw me and I was able to get inside, so I hid myself and waited. I heard you come in, but I stayed hidden to make sure that the man who carried your baggage had gone. And then, before I could come out, you — you — "

Mason smiled. "There's no need to go on from there. I'm sorry that I embarrassed you. Just go on and tell me about Panjit Sangh. I assume that you must be a very good friend of his."

Shareena nodded, and looked embarrassed again. "Panjit and I are — are very close. He is a very brave man." She looked up. "You will help him, Captain Mason? Panjit always spoke so highly of you. He often talks about the North Eastern frontier and how you both fought to stop the war between India and the Chinese, about those stupid villagers and those awful monks from the monastery of Karakhor. He feels that only you can help him now. You must help him."

"I'll do my best," Mason promised. "But I have to know the whole story before I can do anything."

"Of course — "

Her hands played nervously and Mason gave her a reassuring smile.

"Start at the beginning," he suggested. "It's usually the best place, regardless of how long it takes to get to the actual point. You've got the rest of the afternoon to tell me."

Shareena managed a smile in response. She was silent then for a moment, and

Mason realized that he was disturbing her by wearing nothing but a towel. He decided to give her more time while he took his clothes into the bathroom and dressed, but she again began to talk and so he waited.

"You must know that Panjit is no longer in the army. His leg was broken in an accident and the army has no room for crippled Lieutenants. If he had been an older officer he might have got a desk job, but he was too young. He was discharged. He came to Kashmir, to Srinagar, because it was better for his health, and because he wanted to write a book. That was where I met him. He needed someone to help him type his manuscript. There is also another woman, and this is where the story starts.

"The other is a woman named Vandana." Shareena's voice became bitter. "She became very friendly with Panjit, and she pretended that she had an interest in his book. The book was to be a military history of India, her wars and her battles, and biographies of her most

35

famous soldiers. Panjit had studied these things when he had decided to make his career in the army, and after he was discharged it was still the only real knowledge that he possessed. However, Panjit gradually began to realize that this woman was mostly interested in his own experiences of fighting on the North Eastern frontier. She asked him many questions concerning the Indian tactics in mountain warfare, and how the Indian troops had been deployed against the Chinese. Panjit then began to suspect that she was a spy, and that she was deliberately pumping him for information which would be of use to the Chinese troop commanders if they were to again attack over the Himalayas, either in the north east or in Kashmir and Ladakh."

Shareena glanced up at Mason and no longer seemed aware that he was naked under the towel. She said even more bitterly, "I told him to turn her over to the Indian authorities. To have nothing more to do with her. But Panjit was stubborn. He said that spying could work two ways, and he was convinced that he was more clever than Vandana. He believed that if he kept up his association with her he could ultimately learn more about her and her contacts with the Chinese. He had been very unhappy when he had been forced to leave the army, and I think he needed this battle of wits to restore his faith in himself, to prove that he was still capable of serving his country. I argued with him, but he had made up his mind, and there was nothing more that I could do.

"All this happened many weeks ago. Panjit was unable to find any actual proof, but he became fully convinced that Vandana was a spy, and that she was linked with some kind of spy network that has been operating in Kashmir and Ladakh. It was difficult for him, because his crippled leg made it impossible for him to follow her, or to make any active moves against her. And he refused to let me interfere. I told him repeatedly to pass his suspicions on to the proper authorities, but then he told me that he had good reason to suspect that there was a traitor either in the Indian Military Intelligence or the Military Police in the Kashmir area. I do not understand most of this, but Panjit believed that Vandana was under the protection of someone high up in one of those two departments. He felt that if he handed the matter over she would be warned and would escape.

"Finally he decided to write a letter to one of his old army officers in Delhi. He felt that he could trust this man to pass it on to Indian Military Intelligence outside Kashmir. However, even after he had written the letter he was still uncertain that he was doing the right thing, and so he delayed posting it until it was too late.

"Six days ago some unknown person broke into the army camp at Srinagar. Two Indian sentries were murdered, and some important filing cabinets were broken open. Nothing was stolen, but the papers had all been disturbed and the police believe that the papers had been photographed. Whoever was responsible escaped unseen, but he left behind him one clue. The clue was the last page of

Panjit's letter to the army officer here in Delhi, complete with his signature across the bottom. Panjit did not even know that the letter had been stolen from his desk until the police showed it to him, and then they refused to believe him. It was — it was a very vague letter, for he had deliberately phrased it so that he did not fully commit himself. He had asked that it be passed on to the right authority and explained that he had important information that might be vital. Without the rest of the letter he could have been offering information to anyone."

She paused again, making a definite attempt to keep the bitterness out of her voice.

"Panjit denied any knowledge of the raid on the army camp and the death of the two sentries. The police did not believe him, but because of his crippled leg they had to admit that he could not personally be responsible. They questioned him for a long time about the letter, but he made up a story that it had been intended for a publishing house in

Delhi and that the information concerned his book. It was a very poor story, but he felt that it would be a mistake to accuse Vandana without any positive proof. That was when he decided to send a cable to you. He was desperate, and he knew that if it was possible you would come. He did not want you to come direct to Srinagar because you would become known to the police and to his enemies whom he was sure would be watching you. So he asked you to come here to Delhi. Then the police returned and told him that he must not leave Srinagar until they had made further enquiries. They were not satisfied, and believed that he was directly involved with a conspiracy to steal Indian defence secrets and pass them on to an enemy. They told him he was under open arrest and confiscated his manuscript and all his papers."

Mason frowned. "What about his army friend here in Delhi? Why didn't he rewrite that letter and post it off with all the facts?"

Shareena answered wretchedly, "Because the man was not exactly a friend. He was simply one of Panjit's superior officers. Panjit knew that he was honest and loyal to India, but after he had been placed under arrest and accused of spying he felt that his officer would no longer be inclined to believe his story. You were his only hope."

"I see." Mason reached and touched her shoulder. "Stop worrying and let me think things over. I'll put some clothes on at the same time."

He gave her a smile, and then gathered up clean clothes and went into the bathroom. He closed the door behind him and indulged in a brief shower before he dried and dressed. His movements were mostly mechanical, reflex actions, and his mind was busy examining and probing the girl's story. He finally came to two conclusions. One, that he believed her, and that everything she had told him she sincerely believed to be the truth. And two was that he still had confidence in Panjit Sangh, he was still sure that his friend would not be guilty of any disloyalty to India. However, the situation was far more complicated

41

than he had expected, and he wondered whether Kendall would still be willing to let him risk becoming involved.

One point was clear. His next move was to Srinagar, to obtain a more detailed analysis of the situation from Sangh himself. Kendall had at least foreseen that far, and had raised no objections. Mason zipped up his trousers, combed his hair, and thoughtfully studied his own reflection in the mirror. Then he decided that he could always placate Kendall by making his wife a gift of the cashmere shawl. The air was cooler now that the afternoon was getting late, and he casually knotted a red silk cravat into the open neck of his light grey shirt. It gave him a deceptive, sporting air which he liked to practise and feeling fully attired he returned to the bedroom.

Shareena still sat where he had left her, but she stood up when he appeared. He made her sit down again and then said, "I shall have to go to Srinagar. There's nothing that I can do from here. But I don't think that it would be advisable for you and I to return together. It's just possible that someone will be watching the airport for your return, especially now that you've slipped away from the man who was following you. I'll go to Srinagar alone and — " He was going to say contact Panjit Sangh, but suddenly he knew that that would be the wrong move. Instead he said quietly, "And try to contact this woman Vandana. Tell me where to find her, and how to recognize her."

Shareena said, "She has a large houseboat on the Dal Lake. It is one of the big luxury boats and is named *Shalimar*. Vandana is an Indian woman, but she is not Kashmiri. She is too tall. She is Hindu, and sometimes wears the mark of Shiva. You can recognize her easily by her jewels. No other woman in Srinagar wears so many jewels. She has bracelets and earrings, and rings upon all of her fingers. She is too rich to be good, I think she is a very evil woman."

Mason smiled. "From that description I should find her easily enough. Now do you think you can describe the man who followed you?"

She hesitated, less certain this time.

"He was Indian. There was nothing very exceptional about him, except that his face was very thin. It was a starved face, like a face from the famine areas, except that he was not starved. Can you understand? His eyes were very deep in his head, always staring. On the plane I could feel them staring."

"I can understand." Mason frowned, and then went on. "If this character is still at your hotel I don't think it is safe for you to go back. I can't take you with me, and with Delhi in such an unsettled state I don't like to leave you here alone. So what am I to do with you? Whatever we do I have to get you settled somewhere before the six o'clock curfew."

Shareena said definitely, "I want to return to Srinagar. I understand that it will be best if we do not return together, so I shall go by train to Pathankot, and from there take the bus to Jammu and then Srinagar. It will take two or three days, so I shall arrive long after you and by a different route."

Mason smiled. "That's a sensible idea.

I can understand why Sangh trusted you to meet me. But where will you stay tonight?"

"At the station. Once I have purchased my ticket for tomorrow's train I can book a retiring room for the night. There will be no difficulty. I left only a small overnight case at my hotel which is not important."

"Fine," Mason approved. "You can write for your case from Srinagar. Any explanation will do for the hotel."

He turned away to the window and stood for a moment looking down into the hot dusty streets. There were a lot of people about, mostly youths clustered in agitated groups. Cars and motor vehicles were few but there were plenty of scooter-taxis, cycles and trishaws. Police in steel helmets patrolled in pairs and broke up the larger gatherings on the pavement, while farther down the road were three scrawny but arrogant cows nosing in the gutter. The sacred mother symbol of the Hindus. There were very few women visible, and even the beggars appeared to be staying under cover. Flies buzzed, and although the worst heat of the day was receding the atmosphere seemed to simmer. Mason turned back to the girl and said, "I think I'd better escort you to the station. There's just time for me to get you there and be back before the curfew."

4

Violent Streets

They left the hotel together and Mason was faintly amused by the bewildered stare of the young clerk at the reception desk. He excused himself for a moment and then left Shareena standing by the door as he went across to the desk. He told the clerk to telephone Air India and reserve him a seat on their next flight to Srinagar, and passed him a five rupee note for service to forestall any questions. He returned to take Shareena's arm and steered her neatly out of the hotel.

There were no taxis to be seen in the street outside and they stood for a moment on the pavement. An over-loaded bus lurched past and a couple of battered lorries. A hopeful trishaw owner pedalled up beside them but Mason waved him away. He turned towards Connaught Place, still hoping

47

for a taxi, but none appeared. Another trishaw swerved towards him and then a small scooter-taxi roared into view. Mason compromised and shouted for the scooter.

He helped Shareena to step up into the tiny, two-seater cab and then squeezed in beside her. The scooter was an ancient Lambretta, and its rider an old man with a few grizzled bristles of white beard. He twisted round in the saddle to look at them and Mason told him to take them to the railway station. The wrinkled nut face still looked blank and Shareena added, "Delhi main railway station. There are three," she explained to Mason as the old man kicked his scooter into life, and then they were roaring off.

Ordinary taxis appeared now that it was too late, big black saloons driven mostly by Sikhs. The traffic thickened and the first set of traffic lights told them that the Lambretta's clutch was dying a rusty death, while the brakes were badly in need of some kind of distant early warning system. Their driver seemed unconcerned.

They had to pass through Connaught Place, the business and shopping centre of New Delhi, and Mason felt that it was just as well that they were heading in the opposite direction from the Parliament buildings. He had a feeling that the streets could explode again at any moment, and Parliament would be the first target of the mobs. Then he remembered that Parliament had been attacked yesterday and would certainly be heavily guarded by the police. Today violence could break out anywhere. Shareena sat nervous and silent by his side as they rattled around the bright green lawns of Nehru Park, and Mason decided that a little conversation was necessary. He doubted if he could distract her mind and so he brought the subject out into the open.

"Tell me about the cause of the riots," he said. "I'm not sure that I fully understand this business about the sacred cow."

Shareena seemed a little startled by his question, but then recovered herself and answered, "All cows are held sacred to the Hindu religion, they are worshipped

49

as the symbols of motherhood. But now there is a situation in which thousands of cows are roaming the streets unchecked, in Delhi and in every other city and town in India, while in Bihar and other areas whole sections of the population are dying of famine. The more modern members of our government wish to slaughter some of the cows for meat, but the Hindu priests are fanatically opposed to the suggestion. In ten of our states the slaughter of cows is totally banned, but the priests want the ban extended to all India."

"But why has the whole thing boiled up at this particular time?"

"I don't know. I think perhaps because of the national elections which are to be held in three months time. The priests hope that those members of the government who are in favour of cow-slaughter will not be re-elected."

"And in the famine areas they will still starve. That's pretty sad for India." Mason kept his tone casual but he was interested in her response. Shareena was clearly educated and intelligent, and he wondered on which side she would make her own stand.

She looked directly into his face for a moment, and then said quietly, "The Hindu is a fatalist. He is humble before destiny. If the gods intend him to starve, then he will starve, and there is no excuse for killing the sacred cow." She hesitated, and then finished, "There are Indians who believe that we must progress, but religion and fatalism are hard enemies. Together they are almost unbeatable."

Mason nodded wryly in agreement, and then asked, "Does the same situation exist in Kashmir?"

Shareena shook her head. "No, the Kashmiris are ninety per cent Moslems. Our problems are of a different kind."

While they talked they had left the prosperous, modern heart of the city behind, and the scooter-taxi was now bouncing through the narrower, more cluttered area of Old Delhi. Mason was alert despite his smile and the easy manner with which he maintained the conversation, and he noticed that although the streets had become more crowded the traffic had become less. There were still buses running, but private cars and taxis had almost disappeared. He remembered the burned-out car that he had seen on the road in from the airport, and had an uneasy suspicion that most car owners were probably keeping their vehicles safely under lock and key in their garages. The crowds also conveyed their own subtle warning. They were noisy and jabbering, as he had expected them to be, but there was no flow of movement along the pavements and the noise came from agitated groups. Most of the trishaw cyclists had stopped to join in the discussions instead of searching for business, and frequently their miniature taxi swayed dangerously as their driver slowed or swerved to avoid groups that had overflowed into the road. Mason glanced at his watch and saw that it was sixty-five minutes to the curfew time, and felt that he would be glad when they had reached the station.

They had exhausted the subject of the sacred cow, and there was no inclination to talk of anything else. Shareena was nervous again, sensing the unsettled atmosphere of the streets. The cramped little two-seater cab forced them to sit close together, and Mason could feel the faint tremble in her body. She was small and vulnerable, and he was tempted to put an arm around her shoulders. At the same time he felt a faint twinge of envy towards Panjit Sangh.

The outbreak came suddenly. There was a muffled chorus of noise from up ahead that swelled quickly in volume. The smashing of glass reached them from a distance and the groups on the pavement began to jabber even more excitedly and rush into the road. Their ancient driver bawled frantically as he had to wrench his handlebars from side to side to miss the running pedestrians, and then he grated through the gears and skidded to a stop. His front wheel caught the heel of a running youth and tumbled him into the gutter, but the boy scrambled up and ran without stopping to argue. The old man yelled angrily, but when he was ignored he stood upright on the footrest to see over the heads of the crowd.

Shareena sat rigid, but Mason quickly leaned forward through the open door of the tiny cab. He straightened up with his head above the roof and snapped at their driver to sit down and stop blocking his view. The old man was prepared to argue, but after twisting round to look at his passenger he decided ungraciously to sit. At the end of the street Mason could see a large crowd advancing towards them, shouting and waving a handful of paint-daubed, unreadable banners. A group of four steel-helmeted policemen were backing up before the mob, shouting in return and brandishing their white-painted riot sticks in agitated warning. One of the policemen began to blow shrilly on a whistle and the mob pressed them harder, at a fast walk, then a trot, and finally breaking into a triumphant run. The crowds who had flooded into the street began to scatter with yells and cries, some of them running to taunt the policemen from behind and then join up with the mob, and others simply running away.

Mason ordered their driver to turn

back. The old man was flustered and the Lambretta had stalled. It took him a few moments to kick it back into life and by then the street was filled with fleeing Indians hurrying past. The scooter-taxi jerked forward and only the nimble movements of the runners saved the old man from committing mass murder as he ploughed through them in a sweeping turn. The scooter swayed crazily and the off-side wheel of the trailing cab lurched up and then crashed down again from the curb. Shareena was pitched hard against Mason's side and this time he did tighten one arm about her shoulders to prevent her from falling out. He glanced behind and now the crowd had split so that he could see the advancing mob without standing up to look over their heads. The mob was coming up fast, still shouting and yelling, but the four policemen had vanished. Mason guessed that they had probably been chased up some side street, or else they had sought the safety of the shops and buildings lining the road. Then the scooter shot forward as the old man crashed through his gears, and the engine gave a deafening roar as he wound open the throttle. Behind them the mob was swallowing up the groups on the pavement and scores of chanting voices were howling the words "Mother Cow! . . . *Mother Cow*! . . . *MOTHER COW*! . . . " and repeating them over and over again.

Their way was blocked by the uncertain runners in the street ahead, and their driver was cursing and shouting as he juggled through the gears and twisted at his handlebars to find a way through. However, they were staying ahead of the mob and Mason saw no cause for any panic. Shareena said frantically, "Captain Mason, what — "

"Call me Paul," he interrupted. It seemed as good a time as any to be calmly informal. They were thrown forward with a jerk as the old man had to brake sharply and he added, "And don't worry."

He smiled as the Lambretta snorted forward again and the smile was effective. Shareena made a brave response and then the whole effect was spoiled as their driver suddenly decided to take a fast left hand bend into a side street. The move was unexpected and afterwards Mason was never sure whether their driver had simply been trying to turn away from the danger area, or whether some sense of duty had caused him to try and circle back towards the station. The manoeuvre was so abrupt that the scooter-taxi all but overturned, and a luckless Indian with shirt-tails flying was bowled aside as the cab swung into his path. Shareena was almost thrown out, and only Mason's tightening grip prevented her from being pitched face-first on to the hard paved street. The tyres screeched and skidded and then the Lambretta straightened up again and the engine roared as it careered through a yelling mass of scattering people.

Mason saw an old beggar go sprawling in the gutter, groping helplessly for his stick and his pathetic tin of spilled coins. A fat Hindu in a western suit toppled backwards into a shop front and tore down a hanging assortment of cheap clothes, while a screaming woman frantically dived to scoop up a pair of even louder screaming children. Their driver panicked and charged into another yelling crowd, and only then did he realize that he was heading straight into the path of another close-packed mob of advancing demonstrators. He slammed on the brakes and the Lambretta skidded sideways as he tried to turn back, and in the same moment another of the flying scooter-taxis rammed into the back of them.

There was a shattering crash. Their own scooter-taxi spun round in a violent, rending circle, and their ancient driver was hurled forward from the saddle. The whole thing tipped up and crashed down on its side and Mason was flung heavily on top of Shareena, cutting off her scream of alarm. The engine of the Lambretta roared lustily, its back wheels spun futilely until it stalled and there was silence but for the jabber of the crowds.

The taxi-cab was on its side, but as there were no doors Mason had no difficulty in struggling upright. Shareena was groaning and gasping underneath him, but apart from being badly shaken and winded she was unharmed. The driver of the second scooter-taxi had been flung forward across his handlebars and lay there groaning loudly, while their own driver was picking himself out of the dirt of the gutter. His movements were very slow and there was blood running from a long graze on his arm. The collision had also knocked down several by-passers and an angry crowd closed around the scene, shouting and waving their fists.

Mason helped Shareena to stand and together they stepped out of the wreckage. The crowd backed up but did not part to let them through. Both drivers were too dazed to hear any argument, and the anger of the crowd was directed at the two passengers. Mason was alert for the first movement towards him and when it came he deliberately stepped away from Shareena.

The rush came abruptly and Mason knew that he had to fell the leaders or be beaten up. He recognized the first man as the fat Hindu who had been knocked into the shop-front a few seconds before the crash, and he hit the man with a terrific, lifting right hook that snapped back his head and sent him spinning. His hand came back again almost in the same movement in a fast judo chop that cut down a second man who had darted in from the side. His left foot lashed out and he kicked a third assailant squarely in the groin. His left hand was held flat, deadly as a knife blade, and ready for a stiff-fingered thrust to a throat or solar plexus, but it was unneeded. The man with the kicked groin was screeching loudly as he doubled up on his knees, and the fat Hindu and the smaller man both lay writhing in the dust. The crowd melted back in sudden silence and there was no one bold enough to make a fourth attack.

The demonstrating mob was getting close and Mason grabbed Shareena's arm and hustled her forward. The circle of Indians around the scene of the accident parted to let him through, and he spared a grateful thought for the tough Commando Sergeant who had long ago taught him the basic tricks of unarmed combat. He knew that if he had not been capable of dealing ruthlessly and effectively with the spear-head of the mob then the situation would have been much uglier.

No one tried to stop him and he hurried Shareena back to the main road. They reached it and found that they were still fifty yards ahead of the first mass of demonstrators, and quickly turned left to stay ahead of both groups. They began to run, but Shareena was hampered by the full length sari that wound closely around her legs, and Mason realized for the first time that he had received a bad knock on the knee when their scooter-taxi had crashed. It began to hurt and made him limp badly.

Behind them the two mobs of demonstrators joined together as the second band emerged from the side street from which Mason and Shareena had just escaped. There was a mighty uproar of cheers and shouting, and a confused mingling which slowed both mobs down and gave the two fugitives a chance to increase their lead. Grinning Indians watched them go past, but were mostly interested in the demonstrators coming up behind.

A party of excited youths on the pavement forced them to detour out into the road. They circled the group but as they tried to regain the pavement Shareena slipped on some of the filth that littered the gutter. She cried out as she fell and her face twisted with pain. Mason helped her stand once more, but she too was limping and he saw that she had wrenched her ankle. He looked round then for some hope of refuge, for with both of them limping they would be too slow to keep ahead of the demonstrators. However, there was nothing. No side streets, and already the shops were hastily being closed. From behind came the sound of windows being smashed, and looking back Mason saw that the two groups of demonstrators had re-formed and were beginning to advance again. The chanting voices echoed above the sounds of violence. "Mother Cow! . . . *Mother Cow*! . . . *MOTHER COW*! . . . "

For the moment they had to keep going, but they had barely started to stumble forward again when another outbreak of noise came from ahead. People were again scattering and running in all directions, and Mason expected to see another mob of rioters. Instead he caught a glimpse of white steel helmets, and a chorus of whistle blasts identified a heavy force of police moving to break up the demonstrations. Mason bundled Shareena into a nearby doorway and stood there panting. He tried the door but it was locked.

In the street passengers were spilling out of a trapped bus and adding to the confusion of dodging bodies. Bobbing turbans, flapping shirt-tails and brown legs were darting everywhere and the uproar became deafening. There were frantic screams as the weaker spirits sought for shelter and howls of anger from the approaching mob as they saw the advancing wedge of police uniforms. The vanguard of the demonstrators was made up mostly of youths, spurred on by a handful of withered old men with staves. Their advance became a howling charge and there was a complete disorder of pitched battles and running fights. The policemen lashed out savagely with their riot sticks, and for a few moments they were simply knocking their opponents down and making no attempt to make any arrests. A fusillade of stones and bottles showered through the air, and Mason saw one constable toppled by a direct hit in the face. A dozen demonstrators were knocked back bleeding and the charge became a retreat.

There was nothing that Mason could do except crouch in the doorway and try to protect Shareena from the flying missiles. Mercifully the mob had no interest in them and they were unheeded in the general battle.

After the first clash the two sides drew back, the police trying to re-form. The battleground lengthened and the demonstrators retreated to a safe distance and continued to hurl abuse and stones. The police officer in charge bellowed an order and his men drew their revolvers and began firing over the heads of the crowd. The shots were ordered and precise, but the sound brought pandemonium to the crowd. The mob began to disintegrate, and an old man wrapped in a single, grubby white robe waved his stave desperately and screamed aloud as he tried to rally them.

Mason looked behind him at the closed door and wondered if he could break it down, and in the same moment splinters flew into his face as a bullet slammed into the woodwork. He ducked and cursed, and then a second bullet ricocheted from the pavement and again from the wall.

The angle of the shot was wrong. The first bullet might have been a stray from one of the police revolvers, but the second had most certainly come from above and from somewhere on the opposite side of the street. Shareena's face was now a picture of terror, and Mason realized that she had real cause to be afraid.

Someone was trying to murder them in the general confusion of the rioting.

5

Skirmish

Mason crouched, breathing in dust and the scent of violence. He was sweating and he could feel Shareena trembling as he gripped her shoulders. The doorway provided a minimum of shelter from the revolvers of the police and the missiles of the crowd, but left them wide open to their intended assassin on the far side of the street. A few yards away a black saloon car had been abandoned against the curb. Already its windows had been broken and its tyres slashed, but it offered a momentary refuge and Mason moved fast towards it. He half pushed and half dragged Shareena along with him, and as they left the doorway a third bullet ploughed into the woodwork.

They ducked breathlessly behind the car. A stone clanged off the metalwork and in the same moment the hard-pressed police fired another fusillade of warning shots. A bullet screamed off the roof of the car and Mason knew that again it had come from across the street. He was sure now that their enemy was positioned behind one of the upper windows, and he was taking full advantage of the perfect cover offered by the riots. If he was successful then their deaths would almost certainly be put down to accidental bullets from the police revolvers.

Shareena said desperately, "Paul, those shots — someone is shooting at us. What is happening?"

Mason said harshly, "I can only think of one answer. Your friend with the starved face. You didn't give him the slip after all. He must have followed you to the Orient Hotel, waited for you to come out and then followed the two of us in another taxi. Somehow he's kept track of us, and now he's trying to murder us in the general confusion."

"But how — how could he follow us, in all this?"

"Quite easily. I was so busy trying to get us out of this that I didn't even think

67

that we might be followed. All he had to do was run along behind and keep us in sight. You and I are an obvious couple, while he's just another Indian in a street swarming with Indians. The moment he saw us dive into that doorway he saw his opportunity. He knew we'd be pinned down for a bit and so he had time to find a vantage point opposite where he could safely start shooting."

The tumult of noise almost drowned his words and stray stones from another shower of missiles aimed at the police rattled down on to the car. A bolder gang of youths surged past and a group of police grappled with them in a series of frantic wrestling matches. The police were now trying to make arrests and attempting to drag some of the ringleaders back into their ranks. Rescue attempts were made and more blood was spilled as both sides clashed heavily. For the moment Mason and Shareena were sheltered by the car, but Mason knew that it was only a matter of moments before someone tried to set it alight and flushed them out. They had to move.

"Keep your head down," he snapped.

There was no time for any further explanation and he left Shareena huddled by the car as he sprang to his feet and charged back at the doorway they had just left. His shoulder crashed against it and the building seemed to shake. He stepped back and slammed his shoulder against the door a second time, and this time it splintered and burst inwards. He fell into the interior of the shop just in time to escape the fifth shot from the would-be killer who had abruptly realized what was happening.

He scrambled to one side and picked himself up. He was in a small shop filled with books and writing materials, and in the semi-darkness he could just make out two nervous brown faces peering at him from behind the counter. One was a pop-eyed youth, but the other, an older man with a winding-sheet white robe and a Nehru cap came towards him spluttering with agitation. Mason pushed him away from the door for his own safety and the man fell. In the same instant one of the shop's wooden shutters was torn away and the window smashed as a flying bottle entered on a streaming flood of sunlight. The shopowner groaned wretchedly and crawled quickly back behind his counter.

Mason had no time for apologies or sympathy, for Shareena was still outside. He moved back to the door, taking care not to expose himself and shouted to her to join him. She came at a stumbling run, knocked and buffeted by the passing mob, and he had to reach out a hand to drag her inside. He drew her into safety and for the first time in five minutes he felt that he could relax to draw a proper breath.

When she recovered Shareena said unsteadily, "Paul, what can we do now?"

"Sit tight," he answered. "We're safe for the moment, and unless the mobs decide to start looting these shops there shouldn't be any more danger." He paused, and then added grimly, "At least, you're going to sit tight. I'm pretty sure I've marked the window from which those shots were fired, and as I don't particularly like being shot at, I'm going after the johnny with the gun. With a bit of luck he'll hang around and hope that we'll pop our heads out into the street again, and if he does then that will be his big mistake."

He didn't give her time to argue but steered her behind the protective barrier of the heavy wooden counter where the shop-owner and his youthful assistant were huddled together. He drew a hundred-rupee note from his pocket and pushed it into the older man's hand.

"This is for the door," he explained. "And also for looking after the young lady. I'm going to leave her here for a few minutes, and if she isn't safe and unharmed when I come back I'll throw you out into the mobs."

The dark face beneath the Nehru cap looked ready to burst into tears, but the brown fingers closed around the note nonetheless. The man nodded without speaking, and then Mason pushed Shareena down behind the counter beside him. Shareena looked helpless and flustered and tried to catch hold of his arm, but

71

Mason was already gone. There was a door at the back of the shop and he passed through it without hearing as she called his name.

Here there were no windows and he could barely see through the musty gloom. There was a stale smell and he guessed rather than saw that he was in a small stockroom. An open door led into an even darker passage, and the face of a frightened Indian woman peeped like a swift ghost from a side room and as quickly vanished. Mason ran down to the end of the passage, found the door latch and let himself out into a tiny, cluttered courtyard. More buildings looked down on every side and the whole area was draped with lines of washing. A tap was situated in the centre of the courtyard and the flagstones were wet.

At first glance there was no way out except to go through one of the other houses, but then Mason saw a narrow alley leading off to the left. He went down it at a run and after thirty yards came out on to a narrow side road. The road was almost deserted except for one or two shop-keepers who were only now putting their shutters up, and two scampering children heading fast for home. There were also two solemn-faced cows, lean grey brutes with wide horns, humped backs, sagging slack bellies and every rib showing through their flanks. Mason showed no respect or reverence but barged between them and sent the shocked animals jostling out of his way. He was followed by a loud, indignant moo, and a shriek of rage from one of the Hindu shop-keepers. Then he turned another corner, drawn by the continuing disturbance of the demonstrating mobs, and ran back to the main street.

The riot was at its height with both sides in complete disorder. Through the running bodies Mason saw several Indians sprawling dead or unconscious in the road, and many more staggering and clutching their cuts and bruises. Others were groping to find stones and missiles, and sixty yards up the street to his left he could see that the black saloon car which had temporarily served himself and Shareena as a shield was now on fire. He hesitated for a mere instant, no longer certain that he had been right to leave Shareena unprotected in the shop, but then decided that it was too late to change his plans. He tensed, waited for a gap, and then plunged headlong into the swirl of running bodies.

He felt that he was far enough down the street to escape being seen by the mystery gunman, but even so he took no risks. He hunched low and twisted through the mob as fast as possible. Half way across he was hemmed in by a throng of white-robed bodies and carried a dozen yards up the road towards the blazing car, and then he shook free of the pack and continued to the far pavement. He received a few startled stares, but the mob was fighting the police and no one seemed to consider him an enemy. Their main object now seemed to be to keep up the howling war cries of "Mother Cow!"

Mason was panting slightly, but his physical fitness was a definite asset and he was only momentarily out of breath. He noted that the police were now confident enough to have stopped shooting, and that they appeared to have singled out most of the ringleaders. An old holy man was the prize in the hottest battle now taking place, his followers trying to free him as two sturdy policemen struggled to drag him away. Mason looked up to pinpoint the window from which he and Shareena had been attacked, and then hurried towards it. He kept close to the shop fronts and the wall, and hoped that his unknown enemy was still watching the far side of the road.

Two policemen suddenly swerved towards him. They were yelling loudly and grabbed at his arms. Having recognized a European they were anxious to get him off the streets and tried to hustle him into the nearest shop. Mason had no time to argue and explain, and even though they had only his interests at heart he was forced to deal with them violently. He shook himself, free, doubled one man up with a stiff-fingered jab to the stomach, and sliced the second man out of the way with a back-handed judo chop. The move took them completely by surprise and they both went sprawling out of his path. Mason ran on the last few yards until he was below the window he wanted, and then he dived into the nearest doorway.

He was in another shop, this one filled with pots and pans and a colourful array of plastic bowls and buckets. An almost black faced Indian with a tiny moustache was busily emptying the cash register and he jumped with alarm as Mason appeared. He started to jabber but Mason cut him short with a sharp command to shut up. The flustered Indian hastily slammed the cash drawer shut and stood with his arms wrapped protectively around the register. His eyes stared fearfully and he opened his mouth again as Mason came towards him, and then Mason said softly but viciously, "I haven't come here to rob you. But stay quiet. If you make a noise I'll throw you and your precious cash register out into the street."

Again the threat was effective and the shop-keeper became silent. Mason pushed past him to a door at the back of the shop, went through and looked for a staircase. He was in another dark, and dusty passage, but he could distinguish a flight of uncarpeted stairs to his left. He moved towards them slowly, listening and wrinkling his nose against the stale smell of trapped air. He could still hear the sounds of the rioting in the street outside, but from above there was nothing.

He started up the steps, treading very carefully on the bare boards. A faint creak came from the third step, but without lowering his full weight he removed his foot and stepped over it to the one above. The staircase twisted and became pitch dark. Mason kept one hand on the wall to guide himself upwards, and felt old wallpaper bulging and peeling away under his searching fingers. Now that he had slowed his headlong pace he could feel the pain of his bruised knee once more. The whole knee was throbbing and he doubted if he could start to run again. The air tasted foul and his mouth was dry.

Another stair creaked, and he froze into stillness. There was no answering sound but he waited a full minute before he moved again. He had to remember that his enemy was armed where he had only his bare hands. If the man was still here.

He reached a small landing, and here there was a dusty filter of light from a small window. Outside it was becoming dusk, but there was still just enough relief for Mason to distinguish two doors. He knelt quietly before the first one, his body tensed like a coiled spring, and carefully he tried the door. It opened and he looked through, ready for a revolver shot to be fired above his head. Instead he found himself face to face with two naked three-year olds who regarded him solemnly from the centre of the floor. One was a boy, one a girl, and they stared at him with black-button eyes.

Mason saw the little girl's face twist into the beginnings of a howl, and he smiled reassuringly and touched his finger to his lips. The child blinked, and Mason carefully withdrew his head and closed the door. Mercifully there was no sound of tears or alarm, and so he moved on to the second door.

He was directly above the shop and he knew that it was from one of these two rooms that the shots had been fired. The presence of the two babies definitely ruled out the first door, and so now he knew that the second had to be the one he wanted. Again he knelt, and crouched there listening.

There was no sound. The chanting of the demonstrators and the echoes of the rioting still penetrated from the street, but this particular building might have been deserted. Mason opened the door as carefully as before. His heart was a slow, solid knock in his chest, his mouth was dry and a thin trickle of sweat moved past his left eye. Nothing happened. Mason pushed the door back and saw that the room was empty.

He stood up and went inside. It was a bedroom with two or three thick mattresses lying on the floor. The top half of the window was down and when he looked through it he could see across the turbulent street to the shop doorway where he and Shareena had taken refuge.

The police had advanced farther down the street and there were mostly white helmets below him now. The blazing car had almost burned itself out, and behind the police two large lorries were busily loading up with arrested rioters. The police were winning and the demonstration was broken up. Directly below a fallen banner had been trampled into the gutter.

Mason turned back to examine the room, but there was nothing more to see. He breathed deeply and the faint sting of cordite touched his nostrils. He was positive then that this was the room, but he had arrived too late. The gunman had left.

He stood undecided for a moment, and then he remembered Shareena. It was just possible that the gunman had gone after her. He hurried out on to the darkened landing and turned back to the staircase, and then abruptly he sensed his danger. His assailant might have made some slight sound as he straightened up in the darkness, or it might have been Mason's own blend of training and instinct that triggered off the warning. He only knew that the man was there.

He twisted, expecting a shot, and yet that same instinct made him throw up his left arm and sway his body backwards. Something like the weighted lash of a silken whip snapped around his wrist and jerked savagely. He stumbled off balance and then closed with his attacker, grappling desperately for a hold. The man wriggled like a human eel and his eyes were obviously much more accustomed than Mason's to the darkness. The brief look into daylight through the window had robbed Mason's eyes of the familiarity he had gained as he ascended the staircase. For perhaps ten seconds they were locked together, and if it had lasted Mason's superior weight and strength would have told. Then a bony knee gouged cruelly into his groin and brought a rush of tears to his eyes. His opponent slipped past him in the darkness and Mason missed his hold. A second later there was another violent jerk on his wrist and Mason was dragged off the landing and went crashing down the staircase on the heels of his fleeing enemy. The bend in the staircase stopped his fall, but by the time he had struggled up again the other man had vanished.

Limping and breathing harshly Mason reached the foot of the staircase and re-entered the ground floor shop. He crossed to the doorway but he was far too late. The unknown man had merged into the rioters and was gone. The street outside was still drowned in confusion, even though the noise and the violence was diminishing, and Mason had to accept that his first skirmish with the enemy had been lost.

He stepped back into the shop and ruefully examined the only clue that was left, unwinding it slowly from his wrist. It was a long scarf of black silk, and he realized that if it had curled around his neck as it had been intended, then his neck would have been broken by the jerk that followed. He folded the strangling scarf carefully and decided to rejoin Shareena.

6

Srinagar

The Indian girl was undoubtedly pleased to see him, and her face showed that she had been badly worried. Almost half an hour had passed before he was able to get back to her, for apart from the time it had taken for him to circle round and come to grips with the unknown strangler he also had to delay a further ten minutes until the street had partially cleared before he could make the return journey. He had no desire to be caught a second time by the two policemen he had been forced to manhandle, and so the delay was necessary. He found Shareena unharmed, and as he entered the book shop she came quickly to meet him.

"Paul," she said anxiously. "What has happened?"

"He got away." Mason said wryly. "But he left this behind. He was waiting for me on the landing and tried to strangle me with it. Either he finds it a more favourable weapon for killing at close quarters, or else he was afraid to attract attention by using his revolver. There was no shooting from the police to cover his shot."

As he spoke he showed the scarf of black silk. There was a tight knot in one corner which he unpicked with difficulty, and then he shook an old-fashioned silver rupee into his hand. The coin was the weight that caused the silk to whip into a tight coil. Shareena stared at it, and then said uncertainly, "A strangling scarf. It is the kind that was used by the Thugs who terrorized all of India during the beginning of the last century." She looked up into his face. "You must have heard of them, they were a secret society who followed the cult of Khali. Khali is the Earth Goddess of Hindu religion, the female manifestation of Shiva." She paused, and her next words came out in a nervous rush. "Paul — those sentries who were found dead at the army camp. They both had broken necks!"

"I was beginning to guess that," Mason said quietly. "This scarf is a perfect method of silent killing, ideal for dark nights and dark stairways."

"But what does it mean?"

"I'm not sure yet." Mason glanced down at the strangling scarf once more, and continued thoughtfully. "The Thugs used a white scarf if I remember correctly, but this one is black. A more suitable colour for killing in darkness, but not in keeping with a religious revival. I think we're merely up against a murderer who finds this a nice, convenient method."

Shareena shuddered, and then asked, "What will we do now?"

Mason frowned and thought it over for a minute.

"We'll go back to the Orient Hotel," he said at last. "Our friend is sharp enough to still be watching us, so I'm definitely not taking you to the station and leaving you there alone. Tomorrow you'll come with me as far as Amritsar, and then we can separate there so that we still arrive in Srinagar by different routes. That won't fool the enemy now, but at least there's no point in making ourselves obvious to the police as well."

He stuffed the scarf of black silk into his pocket and took her arm, and they returned warily to the street. It was nearly empty now and a police loudspeaker was warning that anyone still visible in ten minutes time would be breaking the curfew. Mason turned towards the Orient Hotel and they both walked as fast as they could away from the scene of violence.

* * *

The following morning a taxi took them back to Palam International airport where they boarded an Air India internal flight for Amritsar, two hundred and fifty miles to the north west. There had been no difficulty in booking a second room for Shareena and they had spent a quiet night at the Orient Hotel. Their flight bookings had been confirmed only two hours before take-off, and had given them just enough time to pay a quick visit to the hotel where Shareena had originally stayed. They collected her small suitcase and paid her bill, but when Mason enquired after the mystery man with the starved face they found that he had hastily vacated his room the previous night. Mason had expected nothing less, and so they went directly to the airport.

After the troubles of the previous day New Delhi seemed quiet, and Palam Airport was ordered and serene. The aircraft that awaited them was a short range Fokker Friendship, and as they climbed up the gangway and entered the fuselage Mason carefully noted the faces of their fellow passengers. They were mostly Indians, but none of them had the thin, starved face for which he was searching, and when he glanced at Shareena she shook her head.

The plane took flight, and after an hour of cruising high above the flat, endless plains of northern India they landed at Amritsar, the capital of the Punjab and the home of the Sikhs. Mason wished that he had time to visit the famous Golden Temple, the centre of the Sikh religion, but his mission was too urgent. Instead he spent a last few minutes with Shareena in the transit lounge, and when the plane was ready to fly on he resumed his seat for the flight up to Srinagar. Shareena was to take a bus and travel by road via Jammu, and he felt that from here she would be safe.

On leaving Amritsar the plane flew high over the continuing plain, and without the Indian girl to engage him in conversation Mason had nothing to do but watch the earth passing below. The plain was divided into tiny green and brown squares and dotted with small mud villages. Pools of water reflected the sunlight like signalling mirrors, while along the irrigation channels the sun's rays travelled in brilliant flashes, like molten mercury flowing parallel to the movement of the plane.

A river appeared, a great twisting sprawl of descending silver that was born somewhere beneath the distant, misty cloud. The aircraft followed its course until it had almost soaked away into a wide bed of yellow sand, and then flew on above rising brown hills. Far away beneath the plane's wing Mason saw a white glimpse of the Himalayas, and then the plane was landing at Jammu.

There was a second brief stop, and the passengers waited patiently in the plane for a handful of new arrivals. Then the plane lifted up into the sky once more. It was now heading directly north and the pine-clad hills growing higher below them were dusted white with snow on their northern slopes. The Himalayas were sharp and clear below the starboard wing with their knife-like peaks frozen and glistening against the blue of the sky. The view was practically unchanging throughout the rest of the flight, until at last the aircraft dropped down into a wide, flat-bottomed valley ringed by mountains, the beautiful vale of Kashmir. The journey that would take Shareena the best part of two days had taken a little less than two hours.

As they landed Srinagar was directly in front of the plane's approach, so there was no glimpse of the city from the air. A bus took the motley group of passengers over to the airport buildings, and here Mason submitted to the routine nuisance of having his passport and baggage examined. Another bus owned by Air India stood ready to take the passengers into the city, but Mason chose to take a taxi. The driver was keen to take him to one of the houseboats on the Dal Lake, which were a favourite tourist accommodation, but Mason insisted upon a hotel. The air was cooler here, and he guessed that the nights would be cold upon the lake.

During the short drive from the airport the vale of Kashmir lived up to its reputation as one of the most beautiful spots on earth. It was autumn here, and the trees were covered in all its scarlet, rustic glory. There were thousands of slender, silver-bark chenar trees, small orchards in golden-brown leaf, and huge maples that overhung the road. The outskirts of the city were a dilapidated Switzerland with little brick and wooden houses with overhanging eaves and balconies, all mellowed by age and time. The taxi entered the more modern heart of the city where the streets were a chaos of pedestrians, cyclists, occasional vehicles and scores of horse-drawn tongas, and to his right Mason glimpsed a silver curve of the river Jhelum.

The taxi-driver made a last attempt to persuade him that he should rent a houseboat, but Mason was adamant about a hotel. He stressed a small hotel, for he did not want to be too conspicuous, and finally the taxi stopped outside a reasonably smart building bearing the sign Hotel Jahan. Mason expressed satisfaction, paid off the driver and went inside.

The tourist season had for the most part departed with the summer, and so there was no shortage of rooms. The taxi-driver loitered in the doorway until he saw Mason sign the reception book and take his key, and then he accepted that he was no longer needed and went away. A grinning youth in the uniform white jacket took Mason's case and showed him up to his room on the second floor. The room was clean and tidy, which was all that Mason required.

He gave the boy the expected tip and sent him away. Then he took off his jacket and shoes, laid back on the bed and thought seriously about his next move.

* * *

At this present stage he had only two courses of action. One was to contact Panjit Sangh, consult with his friend and then decide his next move from there. The other was to stay clear of Sangh and attempt to reach the woman, Vandana. The latter course would have been his obvious choice, but if Vandana had sent the man who had followed Shareena, and then tried to kill them in Delhi, then obviously she would recognize him from that man's report. He turned the problem over and over without seeing any but the two alternatives, and then decided that either way he would have to get at the woman to get the truth.

In effect that task would probably be easier now that he did not have to worry about arousing her suspicions. He could safely assume that her suspicions would be already aroused. The only question was whether she would be willing to engage him in a battle of wits. She had already out-manoeuvred Panjit Sangh and he could only hope that she would be confident enough to try. It all depended upon whether she considered him to be any real danger to her interests. If she did then she would need to know more about him, just as he wished to know more about her. If so battle would be joined. Mason smiled at the prospect.

★ ★ ★

He spent that afternoon and the following day in seeing Srinagar, and following the normal tourist pattern. He knew that he was not fooling his enemies at all, but he wanted them to think that he was naïve enough to make the attempt. So far they could only guess that Sangh had sent for him, and he preferred to give the appearance of an amateur rather than that of a professional.

The first afternoon was easily filled, for he had barely finished his thinking when he heard a polite knock on his door. He opened it to admit a small, dark-faced Kashmiri in a western suit and was cordially invited to a tour of inspection of one of the city's wood-carving factories. Having decided to climb on to the tourist roundabout he had no objections, and his benefactor cheerfully drove him into the old part of town in a big grey saloon, and stopped by some tumbledown buildings on the river bank. The factory consisted of two rooms where a small group of shrivelled Kashmiris were carving wooden animals and fruit bowls, and a third room where another group were embroidering carpets by hand. The tour took three minutes, and then Mason was ushered into a large shop stocked with the finished products. He dutifully bought two small carvings and found that he was expected to make his own way back.

He left the wood factory and almost immediately another grinning little man was tagging at his heels. He wore baggy white trousers, an old army jacket, and a pointed astrakhan cap on his head. He announced that he was a guide and Mason hired him for the rest of the afternoon. He was already realizing that the locals were wide awake to the possibilities of the tourist trade.

By the end of the afternoon he had to admit that he would have been hopelessly lost in the bewildering maze of the old city without his guide. The little man led him on a zig-zag course that wended back and forth across the nine bridges of the Jhelum which looped like a lazy snake through the city. Each bridge was supported on old-fashioned wooden struts, and gave long, romantic views of the river, lined with ramshackle wooden buildings and the silver spires of Hindu temples. The streets were narrow and primitive and there was rarely room for a car to pass through, although the horse-drawn tongas managed to penetrate everywhere. The crowds were jabbering and bustling, but seemed more cheerful and energetic than the Indians of the south. The buildings were nearly all wooden and ancient, with tiny open shops and overhanging with eaves and balconies, and apart from the Jhelum itself there were scores of canals and branching waterways, all filled with moored houseboats and rafts of floating logs. Mason decided that it was a hotch-potch of the world. A crazy blend of the canals of Venice, the floating river communities of the east, the lumber towns of Canada, and the noisy peoples of India, all dumped together in what had rightly been called the Switzerland of Asia.

He finally had to call a halt to his eager little guide, for it was getting dark and he was beginning to feel exhausted. They rode a tonga back to the hotel Jahan, where the Kashmiri promised to wait on him the following morning, and Mason wearily went inside to eat. He spent the evening at the hotel bar, and then retired early to bed.

The following morning he kept to his decision to waste another day before making some deliberately clumsy attempt to contact Vandana. The details he had yet to work out, but it would have to be clumsy to be in keeping with his role of the inexperienced amateur. The little guide in the army jacket and the astrakhan cap appeared promptly after he had eaten breakfast, and again Mason gave the man free rein. There was a brief consultation with the manager of the hotel, and without Mason's help it was decided that he would be taken on an excursion to the top of the thousand foot high hill of Sankaracharya, where an ancient Hindu temple overlooked a panoramic view of the city and the lake. The idea suited Mason perfectly, and he took along a pair of binoculars.

They climbed up a steep, zigzagging path with the guide leading the way. In places it was quite rugged and Mason made no attempt to hurry. They were soon climbing above Srinagar, but at first the valley and the encircling chain of the Himalayan peaks were obscured in the morning mist. Gradually the air became clearer until the snow-caps became distinct against the blue sky, and on the far side of the city a dominating hill crowned by a large military fortress emerged into slow detail. More directly below the slender chenal trees formed a forest of silvery spears thrusting above

97

the rooftops around the outskirts of the city, and a long armada of houseboats lay like elaborate white toys along the floating gardens that fringed the Dal Lake.

Mason called a halt and spent ten minutes using his binoculars. He looked in all directions for the benefit of the guide, and even gazed down on the right hand side of the ridge where the Jhelum coiled in wide sprawling curves before circling behind them to narrow and lose itself through the obscuring maze of the old city where they had walked the previous day. Then he turned his glasses back to the left hand side of the ridge, and looked down upon the lake and the houseboats. He searched for the name *Shalimar* but failed to find it.

As they climbed higher their route was lined by rocks and boulders, small pines and autumn coloured trees. Then the path rounded the last shoulder of the hill and they could look down upon the widening expanse of the lake, reflecting the beauty of the far mountains.

Mason paused for breath, and his guide stood back, grinning proudly and waving his hand to indicate the splendour of the wide views on all sides. The crest of the hill was flat except for one last rising pinnacle on which stood the small, grey stone temple. Close to the temple stood a small party of Indian tourists with their guide, and on the far side of the hilltop a tall woman in a bright red sari stood alone. Mason noticed her immediately and he saw the sunlight sparkle off the jewellery at her wrists and throat. He remembered Shareena's description and very slowly he smiled.

It was not necessary for him to seek out Vandana, for his enemy had chosen to make the first move.

7

The Jewelled Lady

For a moment Mason watched the woman in the red sari, her back was towards him and she was looking down over the far reaches of the lake. Her raven-black hair was drawn back into a large, glossy bun at the nape of her neck, a style almost universally favoured by Hindu women, and her stance and carriage told him that when she turned he would see a face of unusual beauty. Her poise was that of complete confidence in her own femininity.

Casually Mason glanced at his guide. Now that they had reached the top of the hill his duties had lapsed, and the little man had wandered off to gossip with some of his fellows who were attached to the party of Indian tourists. Mason watched him and came to the conclusion that the little man was innocent, or at the most an unknowing pawn. This was a regular excursion and any guide would have brought him here after showing him the city. For the moment anyway, it was not important.

Mason moved to a better vantage point and spent the next five minutes in silently admiring the distant peaks of the Himalayas. They were now sharp and clear above the mist that still blanketed some of the lower slopes, and the glacial heights were a forbidding barrier against the blue of the sky. Below, the lake was a deep, dark and placid blue, and behind lay Srinagar.

At last he turned and walked across the hill-top. Looking down on the far side he could follow the writhing course of the Jhelum, while in the distance the vale of Kashmir merged into a misty white horizon. Directly below was an army camp, and Mason's thoughts included two dead sentries and the unknown strangler. He turned at last to look at the small Hindu temple on the highest point of the hill, and here his idle ramblings coincided

101

with those of the woman in the red sari.

She was removing her shoes, and without appearing to notice him she started to climb the flight of stone steps leading upwards to the shrine. Mason took off his own shoes, placed them beside hers, and then followed her. At the top it was possible to walk around the shrine, but not to enter into it. The woman in red circled to the left, and Mason moved to the right. There was no hurry and he walked slowly to meet her.

He had to walk three-quarters of the way round the shrine, and he found her leaning on the low wall and gazing out over the valley. He paused before passing her, and she glanced round calmly. Her eyes were dark, almost black, and her dark brown complexion was flawless. Her face, as he expected, was an example of pure Indian beauty. Her glance was brief and then she smiled faintly and lowered her eyes, drawing her body closer to the wall to let him pass. Mason gave her a warm smile and stepped round her, and she returned her attention to the valley.

Find a stupid question, the thought jabbed into Mason's brain, an amateur approach. He looked up at the shrine and said the first thing that came into his head.

"Is this a Buddhist temple, or is it Moslem?"

She looked round. "It is neither. It is a Hindu temple, dedicated to Shiva." Her voice was clear and pleasant, with no trace of the usual mis-phrased and tumbling accent.

He faced her now, and for the first time he noticed the small, vertical paint mark on her forehead. He smiled bashfully and said, "I'm sorry, I get so mixed up with these religions in the east." He paused, and then added, "Excuse me if I'm being rude, but that mark on your forehead, doesn't that mean — ?"

She laughed and nodded. "Yes, it means that I am a follower of Shiva. The Indians who make a small, horizontal paint mark across their foreheads are devotees of Vishnu. Does that answer your question?"

103

"I think so." Mason smiled. "Those are your gods?"

"That is right. Shiva is the destroyer of evil, and Vishnu is the preserver of good, although they are in reality the same being. We worship one God with many faces." She saw the perplexity on his face and explained. "You may draw some slight comparison with your Christian religion, where you speak of God, the Father and the Holy Ghost, dividing into three and yet believing in one Supreme Being. The difference is that in Hinduism we divide not into three but into thousands, although Shiva and Vishnu are the most worshipped."

"It sounds terribly complicated," Mason said.

She smiled again. "But only to a westerner. You are English?"

"That's right. My name is Mason, Paul Mason. I'm staying at the Hotel Jahan for a couple of weeks." He looked at her hopefully.

"My name is Vandana," she said. "My home is in Srinagar. I have a houseboat on the Dal Lake."

She indicated the direction with her hand, and her slim fingers scintillated in the sunlight. She wore a dazzling amount of jewellery and there were rings on every finger. Gold bangles tinkled faintly on her wrist, and there was a linking network of jewel-studded golden chains which gloved the whole hand in magnificent splendour. It was the hand of a Maharanee, and far outshone the glittering sapphire brooch that fastened her sari. He felt sure that every stone was genuine, which meant that she was wearing a fortune merely to climb a hill. That made her a very wealthy woman indeed, and he wondered why she had any need to indulge in the sordid game of spying. The only answer was that she played it for excitement and the thrill of success, which meant that she was obviously successful and consequently dangerous.

They stood for a few moments longer, admiring the view, and then Vandana turned to leave. Mason followed her, and when they came back to the descending steps he moved past her and offered her his hand. She smiled gratefully and accepted. Her fingers were very cool against his palm, and they lingered for a moment after they had reached the ground. An Indian in a black coat and a white turban appeared, seemingly from nowhere for Mason had not noticed him before. He knelt at their feet and helped Vandana to slip into her shoes.

"This is one of my servants," she said. "His name is Zakir. I have just two male servants to attend me."

Having assisted his mistress Zakir turned towards Mason, and Mason allowed the man to help him with his own shoes. He looked down on to the turbanned head as the man tied his laces and for a moment he wondered. The dark face had been thin but not starved, and the sharp eyes had been deeply distrustful. Then he decided that Vandana would not be careless enough to confront him with the man who had tried to kill him in Delhi, even though he had been unable to see his attacker's face in the dark. He looked towards her and smiled.

"I too have a guide somewhere, but as yet he hasn't introduced himself. He just

shows me places and grins all the time."
He paused, sensing that she was ready to
leave, and then asked, "Do you mind if
I walk back down the hill with you. I'd
like to hear more about your Hindu gods.
That's if I'm not being too rude?"

She shook her head. "Of course not.
I am pleased that you are showing such
interest. The only way for the peoples of
the west to truly understand the peoples
of the east is to try and understand
our beliefs, and so I shall be happy to
continue our conversation." She gave him
her arm and they walked back together to
the path that led down the hill and back
into the city.

The little man who was Mason's guide
saw them leave, and hastily left his group
of friends and hurried to join them. He
tactfully fell into step beside Zakir who
was walking a few paces to the rear,
but Vandana's servant was disdainful
of talking to him. The silver buttons
on Zakir's black jacket shone in bright
contrast to the dull brass ones on the
Kashmiri's second-hand army jacket, and
after a few moments the little man fell

another disconsolate pace behind and walked alone.

Vandana was attempting to explain the more complex details of Hinduism, pausing only when Mason had to help her to negotiate the more rugged sections of the path. Mason asked her a host of not too intelligent questions, and concentrated mostly on showing her a cheerful mixture of olde world gallantry and courtesy. It was a technique which he often practised upon women, and which he usually found successful because so few men used the same approach in this modern age. There was a flamboyant and individualist side to Mason's character that made his style seem natural, and he was still wearing the casual clothes and the silk cravat which dressed him for the part. His manner was also an excellent shield for the tougher qualities which made him one of Naval Intelligence's most valuable field agents, and now he played upon one side of his character to conceal the other.

The descent was almost as tiring as the climb up, and half way down they stopped to rest. They were once more over-looking the narrow, inner end of the lake and the city, and Vandana pointed to the distant rows of moored houseboats.

"My houseboat is down there," she said. "It is called *Shalimar*, and with your glasses you should be able to see it."

Mason smiled and took his binoculars from their leather case. He gave them to her and allowed her to find the houseboat for him. She searched for a moment and then handed them back.

"There," she said. "Directly below us. The sixth boat from the left in that first row of houseboats. It is the white one with the green tiles on the roof."

After a few moments Mason was able to bring the boat into focus. It was one of the largest on the lake and he could now read the name on the bows. It appeared to be deserted, and inwardly he wondered whether she had witnessed him when he had unsuccessfully tried to find it earlier.

Beside him Vandana said, "*Shalimar* means the abode of love, did you know that? That is why so many princes and Rajahs bestowed the name upon their private gardens. There are *Shalimar* gardens on the far side of the lake that were laid out by the Mogul emperor Jahangir. They are very beautiful."

She was standing very close beside him, and when Mason looked at her she favoured him with a very frank smile. He knew that she was gently playing with him and he smiled in return.

They rested and their conversation became more general, and after some ten minutes they continued the descent. Vandana gave herself even more willingly to Mason's steadying hands, and when they at last reached the foot of the hill she leaned weakly against him. It was then almost noon and she said openly, "Such exercise always gives me a healthy appetite, and today I am feeling ravenous."

"Then permit me to buy you your lunch," he suggested. "We can take a tonga, and go to whichever is your favourite restaurant."

She hesitated as modesty desired, and then answered, "Thank you, Paul. I'd love to."

Mason dismissed his trailing guide with a handsome tip, and then they hailed a tonga and climbed up into the carriage. Zakir sat in the front with the driver, and at a swift trotting pace they were conveyed back into the city. They alighted at one of the better-class restaurants, and Zakir waited outside while they entered.

The restaurant served western as well as Indian cuisine, and they both decided upon a large mixed grill. Mason felt in need of a large beer, and was just a little surprised when Vandana joined him. Their friendship ripened as they sat at the table, and over coffee she advised him on how to spend the rest of his time in Srinagar. One of her final suggestions was that he must not miss taking a *shikara* on the lake.

"The *shikara* is the gondola of Kashmir," she explained. "To visit Kashmir and fail to ride a *shikara* upon the lake is as much a sin as to visit Venice and fail

111

to make a voyage by gondola along the waterways."

Mason rose to the bait. "It seems the perfect way to spend the afternoon. Will you join me?"

She responded as he expected, a smile, and then a sudden flicker of disappointment.

"I am sorry, but this afternoon I already have an appointment."

He looked hurt. "Tomorrow then?"

Vandana hesitated, and played with her spoon. It was against the rules to rush. Then she looked up and nodded.

"All right, Paul. I shall be pleased to accept. I will arrange for the *shikara*, and send Zakir to fetch you."

For another ten minutes they sipped their coffee and made plans for their trip upon the lake, and then she glanced discreetly at her golden wristwatch. Mason paid their bill and then escorted her outside to where Zakir was patiently waiting. While her servant was calling a taxi she excused herself on the strength of her prior appointment, and thanked him graciously. Mason accepted her hand for a moment, and then watched as she climbed into her taxi and was carried away.

Afterwards he returned to his room at the Hotel Jahan and once more laid down upon the bed to think. He was well satisfied with the way events were moving, but even so quite a lot of careful thinking was becoming necessary.

★ ★ ★

Vandana had no prior appointment. Instead she returned directly to the *Shalimar*. The taxi took her along the lakeside road, and from there Zakir sculled her across the lake itself in a small boat. She had to lift up the lower folds of her red sari as she climbed aboard the houseboat, and she went slowly into the large, main cabin. The interior was richly furnished with rugs and cushions, a comfortable divan and several small, polished tables. On one table stood a white vase filled with orchids, and on another a hand-carved chess set neatly laid out with double

113

rows of ivory pieces. There was a faint scent of spice and an overall impression of tasteful luxury. Vandana stood without seeing any of it, for she too was finding it necessary to indulge in some serious thinking.

There was a footstep behind her as Zakir entered. She turned and her face was hard as she regarded her servant. She said curtly, "Find Kalam. Bring him to me."

The man nodded and moved past her. There was a door at the far end of the cabin and he quietly disappeared. After a few moments there was a soft exchange of voices from deeper within the houseboat, and then a second servant emerged through the half open door. Like Zakir he were a black coat with polished silver buttons, and a pure white turban around his head. He too wore the mark of Shiva upon his forehead, and the two servants might have been twins if it were not for his face. Kalam's eyes were sunk deep in hollow sockets, and his dark skin was drawn tight around the bones of his cheek and jaw. It was the starved face that had followed Shareena to New Delhi.

Vandana said coldly, "I have talked with the man Mason. He acts like a charming fool, and if I could not tell a real man when I meet one I could almost believe him. You made a grave mistake when you tried to kill him in New Delhi. Your orders were only to watch the girl and report. If you had done only as you were ordered I might have had the advantage over him now. Instead you have helpfully proved to him that there is a hostile plot against his friend Sangh. He has no doubts on which I can play to convince him that Sangh might be guilty."

Her face became a frigid mask as she stepped forward, and Kalam tensed. She said icily, "Your mistake would have been excusable if you had been successful. There is no excuse for failure and allowing Mason to reach Srinagar alive."

As she spoke she struck him a vicious blow across the face with the back of her heavily-jewelled hand. The sharp-edged stones made a cruel knuckle-duster that lacerated the dark skin in a swiftly-bleeding mess of open cuts. Kalam reeled away with a sharp agonized cry, but he made no other attempt to escape his punishment.

8

Council of War

Mason spent well over an hour in deep thought. The fact that Vandana had chosen to approach him was all the conclusive proof he needed that his would-be killer from New Delhi had reported, or perhaps even returned to Srinagar. Her interest was aroused, but he sensed that she was an extremely shrewd woman, and he was not certain that he had convinced her that he was the fumbling amateur that he wished to appear. Neither was he at all sure of how the next moves should be played.

He finally decided that before he saw her again he would have to contact Panjit Sangh. He needed to know much more of the events that had led up to Sangh's being placed under open arrest, for he could not continue to operate in the dark. He guessed that he was being watched, but as his cover had been broken before he arrived it did not really matter. What was important was to act as though he did *not* know that his cover was broken, and to make a furtive night visit as though he expected to be able to accomplish it in secrecy. He had to convince Vandana that he was inexperienced, allow her to underestimate him, and hope that she would be confident enough to make mistakes. He had to persuade her that his thinking was one step behind, and yet be one step ahead. It was the psychological game of double-thinking endlessly permutated. It was also giving him a headache.

He forced himself to relax, and with the prospect of a long night before him he managed to steal a few hours of sleep from what remained of the afternoon. He ate a solitary dinner at the hotel, and again spent the evening lounging in the hotel bar. At ten o'clock he returned to his room and took a cold shower to sharpen himself up and wash away the effects of the alcohol he had consumed. Then he relaxed again until midnight.

When he arose he dressed quietly in dark trousers, a shirt and sweater, and a black windcheater jacket. He let himself out of the room by the full length window that opened on to a railed balcony. Below the balcony was a courtyard, and in one corner a tunnel-like passage that led out into the street. Mason climbed over the balcony, hung at the full length of his arms and then dropped. He could have accomplished the move in silence, but he deliberately made a few clumsy sounds, not loud enough to awaken anyone in the hotel, but enough to cause a smile of contempt for anyone who was already awake for the express purpose of watching his room. He glanced around him furtively, and then hurried under the stone archway to the street.

He turned left so that he should not have to pass in front of the hotel and walked briskly. The street was deserted and the night was very cold. Above the stars were brilliantly sharp and clear, like a million gleaming spear points stabbed down through the black canopy of the heavens. He did not look round to

119

ascertain whether he was actually being followed, but he did not think that his enemies would find it necessary. They would guess where he was going.

He remembered the directions that Shareena had given him before they had parted in Amritsar, and found his way to the bank of the Jhelum. The river was dark and silent, shaded by the giant black silhouettes of huge maple trees; the moored houseboats like shadowy Noah's arks taking refuge from the darkness of the night. He followed the river along its southward loop, with the towering hill of Sankaracharya on his left, the Hindu temple invisible on its crest.

It took him half an hour of fast walking to find the small house and garden on the left hand side of the road. There was a small orchard beside it as Shareena had described, and a small nameplate fixed to the gate. The name was *Chenar Vale*. Mason suspected that Sangh was also being watched, but showed no sign of his suspicions as he opened the gate and hurried up the path to the house. It was a wooden building, like a Swiss cottage or farmhouse, and was in a much better state of repair than most that Mason had seen. He stepped up on to a small porch and rapped gently on the door.

He had to knock twice before there was any answer, and then the door was opened. As yet no light had been switched on inside the house, and so he could not see the man inside. He said calmly, "Good evening, Lieutenant. How's life?"

"Paul!" The answer came with a burst of relief, and even after four years there was still a note of youthful excitement. "Paul, come inside. I have been expecting you."

Mason stepped into the darkened doorway and an eager hand guided his arm. The hand released him to close the door, and then a light flooded on. He was standing in what could have been a farmhouse kitchen with a red-tiled floor. There was a large table covered with a white cloth, and two chairs. Blue curtains were drawn across the window, and open shelves of plates and crockery lined the walls. Mason recorded it briefly and then faced his old friend.

He was shocked. That first note of exuberance had been misleading and Panjit Sangh was no longer the carefree young officer he had first known. Mason remembered him as tall and slim, but now Sangh had put on weight, and even seemed to have lost height as he leaned heavily upon a stick. In four years his face had aged ten, and there were lines of worry etched deeply around his eyes. He limped forward, and the hand he extended was firm and warm. He smiled, revealing perfect white teeth, and there was just a glimpse of the handsome young Lieutenant from the North Eastern frontier. He said soberly, "Life is not too good, Paul. At least not at the present." He paused and his face was embarrassed. "Paul, how can I thank you for coming. You were my last, desperate hope, and I asked so much. I had no right to ask at all." Their hands were still gripped fast, and Sangh was reluctant to break the hold. He gripped harder and finished, "Words are not enough."

"And they are not necessary," Mason

answered. He punched Sangh lightly on the shoulder and added, "Civilian life isn't good for you, you're getting fat. How's the leg?"

Sangh relaxed. "The leg is what you would call a bloody nuisance," he said ruefully. "But I am learning to live with it." He smiled again. "But you must come into the next room — Shareena is waiting. She arrived late tonight on the bus from Jammu, and we have both been wondering what has happened to you during the past two days."

They moved into the next room, a living room that was simply furnished and made just a little bit untidy by scattered books and papers. A covered typewriter stood on a small writing bureau, and there was a large bookcase jumbled with assorted volumes and folders of papers. There were two comfortable chairs and a divan that did not match. Shareena stood up from the divan, still wearing her attractive blue sari, and shyly offered her hand. Mason gripped it briefly and said, "I'm glad to see you. I trust you had a safe journey?"

She nodded. "There was no more trouble. It was a long and tiring bus ride, but the mountain scenery is very beautiful."

Sangh moved up beside her, still looking faintly embarrassed.

"Sit down, Paul. Shareena will get you a drink, and then you can tell us what you have been doing since you left Amritsar."

Mason accepted the invitation and he and Sangh sat down on the divan. Shareena busied herself with fixing them drinks, and then drew up one of the remaining chairs to face them. Mason sipped the whisky and soda she had given him and then answered their question.

"I've been exploring Srinagar," he explained. "Just getting the feel of the place and the layout of the city. I've also made contact with your friend Vandana, or rather she has taken the initiative and approached me. We met this morning, had lunch together, and tomorrow afternoon we shall be sharing a *shikara* on the Dal Lake."

Sangh said dubiously, "Be careful,

Paul. I thought that I was more clever than Vandana, and now I am in an unholy mess. Are you sure you were not followed here tonight?"

Mason smiled. "I should imagine that I was, or at least that she knows I am here. She knows, or can guess that I am here to help you, so in actual fact nothing would have been lost if I had come here openly and in daylight. By pretending an attempt at secrecy something might be gained. I want her to be amused by my pointless efforts to deceive her, and then it it possible that I might have the advantage."

Sangh frowned, and looked far from happy. Both he and Shareena had left their drinks untouched. Mason gave them no opportunity to protest, but asked Sangh to repeat everything that he had previously been told by Shareena in New Delhi. He listened carefully but it was virtually the same story, and there was only one new development. When Sangh reached it his voice became grim.

"Yesterday I had another visit from the police. They asked me questions again, exactly the same questions as they asked before. They were insistent that I explained more fully the letter that was left behind at the army camp on the night that the two sentries were murdered. I could not deny that the signature on that letter was mine. They demolished the story I had concocted at first, and so I told them the truth. As I expected they disbelieved that also. They said that it was an attempt to wriggle out of my own guilt by accusing an innocent person. They refuse even to question Vandana, and I am still forbidden to leave Srinagar, pending further investigations."

It was Mason's turn to frown. He thought for a moment, and then asked, "What is it that makes you believe that Vandana has a contact somewhere in the higher ranks of the police, or in Military Intelligence?"

"Small reasons," Sangh admitted. "But together they have convinced me. Many of her questions showed a foreknowledge that could only have come from some other source of information, and I received the impression that they were only asked to test the value of my replies. Also the fact that she expects to succeed with this very old trick of simply planting fake evidence to incriminate me. She is a very intelligent woman, and would not resort to such old methods unless she was certain that she could succeed. And she is succeeding. Someone is pressing this case against me, and at the same time shielding Vandana against my counter-accusations. I am sure of it."

"And you think Vandana is working for the Chinese?"

Sangh nodded vigorously. "Of that there is no doubt."

"Why the Chinese? Pakistan is surely the biggest threat to Kashmir."

Sangh smiled bleakly. "You say that because of the war that was fought between our two countries last year, and the dramatic tank and air battles fought just south of Amritsar. And also because outwardly the problem of Kashmir is a religious one, eighty per cent of the Kashmiri population being Moslem and preferring to become part of Moslem Pakistan. But you should know, Paul, that wars are never fought because of the benefit of the people, those are only the propaganda reasons issued afterwards. The greatest value of Kashmir is that it is a strategic bulwark against China. Together with Ladakh it forms a difficult barrier for the Chinese to cross before they can sweep down into India. We can hold them here where we could never hold them farther south. At present relations between China and Pakistan are good, and if India gave up Kashmir there is no guarantee that the Chinese would not be allowed free access to the south. That is why India must retain Kashmir."

He paused to take the first taste at his drink and then continued, "Unfortunately Kashmir is a rich country, the tourist trade brings in much money. That and its military value are the basic reasons why Pakistan is pressing her claim. You must realize that the headquarters of most of the main rivers that flow down into Pakistan originate here in this part of the Himalayas. That means that in effect we are in a position to contaminate

128

or divert almost the whole of Pakistan's water supply. It is something that will never happen, no Indian government would even dream of such a crime, but Pakistan naturally does not like us to hold this position."

"But you still believe that the Chinese are the biggest danger?"

"They are the greatest danger." Sangh's voice was becoming sharp but he was not aware of it. He leaned forward and his glass almost spilled in his hand.

"Our clash with Pakistan is more recent, but in 1963 the Chinese attacked our frontiers in Ladakh. During the winter of that year our troops fought bitter, freezing battles high in the mountains, but even so we could not prevent the Chinese from seizing two thousand square miles of our territory. Previous to that, in 1962, as you well know, they attacked us on the North Eastern frontier above Assam, and managed to seize and hold large areas of our territory there. They are pushing over the Himalayas into India at every opportunity, and they have openly promised to invade Kashmir from the north if the fighting breaks out again between India and Pakistan. It is called a mutual China-Pakistan defence pact, but what it means is that if India is forced to engage Pakistan again, China will stab her in the back."

Mason said quietly, "I can accept all that. Nobody can doubt that China's population explosion is forcing her to expand. But surely it is still possible that Vandana is employed by Pakistan?"

"No, Paul. The information that Vandana has tried to extract from me would be of relatively little use to Pakistan. My military experiences are of mountain warfare, and of the tactics used to combat the Chinese in the high Himalayas. Such information would be of no use to Pakistani tank commanders operating in the desert."

Mason raised one hand in surrender. "All right, Lieutenant. I'll also accept your reasoning that Vandana is employed by the Chinese. Now tell me how long it is since you have known her, and how much time elapsed before you realized that she was only trying to use you?"

Sangh had to think for a moment, and then he answered.

"I first met Vandana about five months ago, but it was only a few weeks before I began to suspect that her friendship was not genuine. As you have seen for yourself, Vandana is a very rich and beautiful woman, and I would have had to be naïve to think that such a woman could have any lasting interest in a crippled and penniless ex-lieutenant of the Indian Army. Her approach was that she too had ambitions as a writer, and she talked mostly about my book. Naturally I have written nothing that cannot be openly published, and my book is mostly a history of India's past military campaigns, so there was no harm in allowing her to read the finished chapters. After that I saw her once or twice a week, and eventually she began to ask me about the North East frontier, and the fighting of 1962."

"And you told her a little, just to bait the hook, and then tried to uncover something more about her?"

Sangh nodded, and smiled bitterly.

"Shareena warned me that Vandana would prove too clever for me. I should have listened to her." He looked at the girl for a moment, and then turned back to Mason. "Shareena is a wonderful girl, Paul. Without her I should be lost. If I had known that there would be any danger in letting her go south to Delhi in my place, I would never have permitted her to meet you. I have to thank you for taking good care of her."

Shareena smiled, and shyly looked away.

Mason said, "I think she was followed simply to see who she would meet. If the riots hadn't provided such a perfect cover for an attempted killing I don't think there would have been any danger." He paused. "But tell me what you did manage to learn about Vandana?"

"Very little," Sangh confessed. "She came to Srinagar about three years ago, but before that her past is a blank. She told me that she lived in Madras, but I am not inclined to believe anything she tells me. I only know that she is a woman of leisure, with a seemingly

132

unlimited supply of money and jewels. In the winter she often travels south to escape the cold weather, but I do not know where. The spring and summer months she spends on her houseboat on the Dal Lake. She has only two servants, which is surprisingly few for a woman so wealthy. One would normally expect her to have a maid at least, but she keeps only the two men. Of them I have only seen the one she calls Zakir. The other stays out of sight. In all the time I have known her I have been able to discover nothing of the links she must have with the Chinese."

"Have you seen her since you were placed under open arrest?"

"Not at all. Twice I have tried to see her, paying a boatman to take me out to the *Shalimar*. But each time Zakir has refused to let me come aboard, and told me that his mistress is not at home."

Mason asked more searching questions, but there was nothing else that Panjit Sangh could add to his story. They discussed the problem far into the night, examining it from every angle, but at the finish it was still a puzzle. Neither of them could see any definite direction that Mason could take to establish Sangh's innocence and Vandana's guilt. Finally Mason said wearily, "The only course I can see is to play it by ear. To meet Vandana tomorrow as I have arranged, and hope that somewhere along the line she will slip up and give me a lead."

Sangh was disappointed, but he had no other suggestion to offer. Then Shareena said earnestly, "Perhaps if we searched the *Shalimar*. I could go there tomorrow while Paul is taking Vandana on the lake. There would only be the servants to deceive in some way."

Sangh looked horrified and Mason said swiftly, "No, Shareena. You're not to go anywhere near the *Shalimar*. Those servants could be killers. In fact, they probably are."

Shareena looked discomfited, and then Sangh reached out and touched her arm.

"Thank you," he said. "But you have done enough. I would not risk seeing you get hurt. You must leave everything to Paul and myself. Promise me?"

Shareena looked up, and then nodded slowly.

They talked for another thirty minutes, and then Mason accepted a final drink before facing the chill night air and returning to his hotel. Shareena stayed with Panjit Sangh, for her family were not yet aware that she had returned to Srinagar. She had recently finished her last year of training in a technical college, but as she was still waiting to take up employment there were no demands on her time. Mason had offered to see her to her home, but as it was nearly morning she had declined, explaining that it would be less awkward for her to return later in the day and pretend that she had only just arrived from Jammu.

Mason walked alone, and thought about Vandana.

9

The Man from Pakistan

It was nearing dawn when Mason climbed back over the balcony of his hotel, and having regained his room without being challenged he slept until it was almost noon. When he awoke he showered, dressed, and descended to the hotel lounge, where he found that his little guide had been hopefully waiting for him for the past three hours. He felt obliged to give the man another large tip, but impressed upon him that his services were definitely no longer needed, and then sent him away. He turned into the restaurant, refused the proferred luncheon menu, and despite protests that at this time it was impossible insisted upon coffee with toast, fried eggs and bacon.

After his late breakfast he idled away an hour in the lounge until Zakir came to fetch him. Vandana's servant was again resplendent in his silver-buttoned black coat and white turban, and his manner was polite but cool. Mason followed him out of the hotel where a taxi was waiting, and then they drove away towards the Dal Lake.

Mason knew that Zakir would tell him nothing, but it was in keeping with his role of an inexperienced amateur to ask some casual questions. When they had entered the taxi Zakir had opened the rear door for his guest, and then seated himself beside the driver, so now Mason had to lean forward to speak to him. The servant barely deigned to turn his head, and made negative and non-commital replies. Mason sat back as though rebuffed, and allowed an expression of vexation to move across his face, which he knew was reflected in the driving mirror. A few moments later they were stopping by the lake.

Mason paid for the taxi and then followed Zakir down to the water's edge. A *shikara* was waiting, looking very much like a venetian gondola. The boatman was a little Kashmiri wearing baggy white trousers and a grey waistcoat. He carried a long pole and his face was a happy grin that made him the twin brother of Mason's ex-guide. There was room for four people on the cushioned seats below the canopy that was built over the centre of the boat, and Zakir and the boatman steadied the craft as Mason climbed inside. Zakir sat opposite him, causing the *shikara* to rock, and then the boatman poled them out towards the long row of gleaming white houseboats that lay opposite.

As they approached the *Shalimar* Mason decided that to describe it as merely a houseboat was somewhat misleading. A more apt definition would be that of a small, floating palace. There were literally thousands of houseboats lining the lake, the Jhelum and the waterways of Srinagar, but the *Shalimar* was in a class of her own. This section of the lake was clearly reserved for only the highest class boats, but even amongst these the *Shalimar* was outstanding.

Their boatman was careful not to bump against the spotless white paintwork, but when Mason started to rise Zakir indicated that he should stay seated. The servant quickly climbed up a short ladder to the houseboat's deck and hurried away. Mason realized that he was not to be invited aboard and waited.

After a few moments Vandana appeared, and he stood up to steady her as she climbed down into the *shikara*. She greeted him with a ravishing smile and he felt his heart begin to slightly quicken its beat as she settled on to the cushions beside him. She wore a golden sari and bodice that left her midriff bare, and on her feet tiny golden slippers. A snowy white cashmere shawl was draped casually around her bare shoulders, and once again she sparkled with jewellery. Her bodice was cut low and fastened with a yellow sapphire between her breasts. A matching necklace encircled her throat, and once again her right hand appeared to be wholly gloved in precious stones. On a European woman it would have been too ostentatious, garish and gaudy, but on Vandana they seemed natural.

Her dark beauty had been born to be adorned with the jewels of an Indian princess.

Mason said sincerely, "You look magnificent."

"Thank you." She gazed at him in turn, noting the red cravat at the open neck of his crisp grey shirt, and the sharp crease of his casual white trousers. Her survey included his hard-muscled arms and the deep blue of his eyes, and then she added, "You are not exactly unhandsome yourself."

They exchanged smiles, and then she spoke a quiet order to the boatman. The man thrust hard on his long pole and the *shikara* moved gracefully across the lake. Zakir had not reappeared from the *Shalimar*, and they were alone but for the boatman. The sunshine danced on the placid waters and they needed the shade of the canopy. Vandana leaned close against Mason's shoulder, and he accepted the unspoken invitation to put his arm around her. Her dark eyes studied his face as she said, "Tell me something about yourself?"

Mason considered for a moment, and then said, "I'm English, unmarried, and thirty-six years old. I'm tall, not exactly dark, but as you've pointed out, not exactly unhandsome. And at the moment I'm on holiday in Srinagar, and cruising on the lake in a Kashmiri gondola with one of the most beautiful women I've ever seen. I'm enjoying myself, and I think that I'm a very lucky man."

She laughed. "That tells me nothing that I did not already know. And thank you for the compliment. How is it that a man so charming as you has managed to remain unmarried?"

"Perhaps because I am a wanderer at heart. I'm a writer of travel books, and that keeps me always on the move." The story had been prepared to explain away his friendship with Panjit Sangh, and also to give him an indefinite background, and he inserted it smoothly. He did not attempt to elaborate but went on, "I'm not very interesting really. I'd much rather talk about you. Are you married?"

She smiled. "I have been married three times, and each of my husbands was richer than the one before. The last was almost a Maharajah and he was very fond of hunting tiger. One day he fell off his elephant while leaning out of the howdah to make a difficult shot. The elephant was a docile beast but curious. It turned round in order to see what had happened and unfortunately trampled upon my husband's head. He had missed his shot so I had neither a live husband nor a dead tiger. Mercifully he left enough money to buy me all the tiger-skin rugs I might need."

She spoke so calmly that Mason had the uneasy feeling that she just might be telling the truth. He waited a moment, watching the last of the large houseboats glide past as the lake opened out before them, and listening to the soft splashing of the boatman's pole. Then he asked, "How do you spend your time now?"

"By enjoying my leisure. When one becomes very rich there is no need to do anything else. I like Kashmir. The scenery is so splendid and the climate is ideal. Only in winter does it become cold, and then I go south to Delhi. I spend the winter season in enjoying the night clubs and the theatres."

There was a slight breeze now that the lake was widening, and she adjusted her shawl closer around her. On their right was the Sankaracharya hill and they could see the small temple where they had first met high above. Across the lake rose the mountains, rugged pine-clad slopes with snow-capped peaks, and at the foot of the mountains lay the apple orchards, shedding their leaves in a russet carpet. On their left lay the floating gardens of lush green lawns and flower beds, shaded by the graceful chenar trees. The *shikara* was comfortable and barely moving over the still blue waters, and it would have been difficult to imagine a more romantic setting.

Mason said idly, "Is Zakir your only servant?"

"No, I have two servants, but Zakir usually accompanies me when I leave the houseboat. Kalam prepares my meals and undertakes most household duties. I prefer not to surround myself with too many servants, for that tends to make me lazy and spoiled. Zakir and Kalam are enough. They are both Hindu, well-trained and completely loyal. They were provided for me by my last husband."

As they talked the *shikara* had drifted in towards the left shore of the lake, and was nosing gently through a floating carpet of tiny red flowers. The boatman appeared to be half asleep and was putting no effort into his work. Vandana gave him a quiet order and he looked down at them and smiled. He turned the nose of the craft until it bumped silently against the grassy bank.

Vandana said blandly, "The breeze is becoming cool, shall we alight and rest in the sunshine for a while?"

"If you wish."

Mason helped to steady her as she stepped ashore, and then followed her. The little boatman moved quickly to lift out some of the rugs and cushions from the *shikara* and then spread them out upon the grass. Then he saluted cheerfully and began to pole the gondola back into the lake.

"He will return in an hour," Vandana explained.

Mason glanced around him with interest. They were isolated on a small island on the edge of the floating gardens. The silver-barked chenar trees were their only companions, wild flowers grew, and the large, glossy green leaves and white trumpets of water lilies ran riot in the cool channels that separated them from the rest of the gardens. The air was fragrant and drowsily warm.

"Very pleasant," Mason said. "Very pleasant indeed."

Vandana had seated herself on the rug and he lowered himself beside her. Her eyes were amused and her lips barely held back her smile. Mason fingered the sapphire necklace that lay against her dark brown throat, and said softly, "These must be almost priceless. Aren't you afraid to be left alone with a stranger who might rob you."

She smiled and lay back on the cushions, letting the white shawl slide clear of her arms and shoulders.

"Not at all," she answered him. "I

think I can distract your mind from my jewels very easily."

Mason tried to read her eyes, but still there was only amusement. He leaned closer and her lips parted in an expectant smile. She neither responded nor withdrew from his kiss. Her mouth was moist and warm, but without movement. He raised his head again to look into her eyes, and her smile was one of supreme confidence. She said softly, "Stand up, Paul. Stand at the water's edge, and tell me when the *shikara* is out of sight."

Mason hesitated, and then stood upright. She lay at his feet still smiling, and after another moment of hesitation he turned away. The *shikara* was fifty yards distant, still poling slowly towards the far mountains. It changed course and began to disappear around a bend in the lake in the direction from which they had come. The smooth, clear blue surface was now unbroken except for the patches of tiny red flowers, and there was no other human being in sight. He turned back and said, "The *shikara* is — "

The words stopped in his throat. The golden bodice had been discarded and the lower half of the sari had been opened out so that it lay beneath her like a golden sheet. She had unfastened her dark hair so that it tumbled in wild disorder upon the white shawl on which she rested her head, and she was still favouring him with that smile of complete mastery. Her brown body was a complete and open, almost agonizing invitation, naked except for the sparkle of her jewels.

She said calmly, "Have you read the Kama Sutra?"

Mason nodded.

"Then you know the rules. Only kisses and caresses for as long as you can bear it. The ecstasy of love should be savoured and prolonged, and the final act is only the ultimate of so many delights." She held out her arms. "Come to me, Paul. Come to me slowly. But you must only take me fully when the desire becomes an unendurable pain."

★ ★ ★

147

It was an unforgettable hour. Her touch was sure and knowing, a continuous stimulation, while her lips talked a silent, seeking language of ancient erotic wisdom. It seemed that his very being was drowned and glorified in that dark, rapturous, sensually moving body, as she poured upon him all the subtle mystic arts of the East. He possessed her, and yet even more so was he possessed. He loved her, and yet what he gave seemed but a morsel to what he received. At the end of the hour he was spent and could only lay with his face buried in the fragrant beauty of her long black hair. Her hands still stroked and caressed him gently, and she was still smiling.

* * *

When the *shikara* reappeared they were ready to return, and the little boatman steadied his craft as they came aboard. The sun was moving across the western sky and the breeze was becoming cooler. Vandana nestled her head upon Mason's shoulder and once more they began their

148

slow, drifting journey across the lake. She was silent, almost dreamy, which gave Mason time to think, and he had to remind himself strongly that despite what had happened she was still technically his enemy. He made himself look for some sinister meaning behind the fact that she had seduced him, but could find none, and suddenly felt that in this case he was being unjust. Whatever else she might be, Vandana was a woman who needed to be loved, and the interlude on their tiny island had been a truce, and something outside the more subtle battle in which they were enjoined. Even so he felt that he needed to beware.

They returned to the *Shalimar*, and he was faintly surprised when she invited him aboard. The boatman was told to wait and they climbed on to the spotlessly scrubbed deck. Zakir appeared in the cabin doorway, and she informed him that they would take tea. She smiled at Mason and said, "I always take tea in the afternoon. It is the one English custom I enjoy. You will join me I hope?"

Mason nodded, and then she led him

149

into the large main cabin. Zakir had already vanished and there was no sign of the second servant. Mason glanced around the luxurious fittings, and then accepted her invitation to sit upon the divan. She talked pleasantly with no mention of their hour upon the lake, and then Zakir returned with a silver tray bearing the tea service and a dish of sweet cakes. He placed the tray on the small table before them and then withdrew.

Vandana served, and continued their idle conversation, and some twenty minutes passed before there was any further interruption. Then Zakir appeared again in the cabin doorway, materializing like a silent Indian ghost, and spoke a few brief words in Hindu. Vandana looked suddenly confused, and then voices from the lake told Mason that another *shikara* had approached the houseboat. Vandana excused herself and went to the door, and Mason heard new footsteps upon the deck. A loud voice spoke a greeting in English and Vandana answered.

Mason watched with interest, but

remained seated on the divan. A few words were exchanged and then Vandana turned to lead her new guest into the cabin. Mason stood up as she introduced them somewhat awkwardly.

"Paul, this is Lalshar Shafi. He is a friend of mine whom I have known for some time. Paul is a writer who is staying in Srinagar."

Mason murmured some appropriate words and then held out his hand. Shafi hesitated, and he was obviously caught off-balance. He was a well built man in his early thirties, wearing a clean white shirt and trousers. His dark brown face had a suddenly agitated look, and he favoured a slim, pencil-line moustache. He accepted Mason's hand but his grip was uncertain and his dark eyes flickered towards Vandana. He was not a Kashmiri, and Mason felt sure that he was not Indian. The name sounded as though it had originated in Pakistan, and suddenly Mason was sure that Shafi was a Pakistani.

Vandana said, "Shafi owns a small

151

curio shop in the old part of the city. It is close to the sixth bridge. If you pay him a visit I am sure that you can buy your souvenirs at reduced prices."

Shafi managed to collect himself and smiled, "Of course, if you need any wood-carvings, ivory, silks or brocades, you must come to me. I usually rob tourists, but not my friends."

Mason promised that he would do so, and Shafi fumbled in one of his pockets and then gave him a printed business card with the address of the shop. The Pakistani seemed glad to have something to do with his hands, but he could not prevent his eyes from taking another worried look towards Vandana. She seemed to have recovered too and said sincerely, "Paul, I am terribly sorry. I had forgotten that Shafi had arranged to call upon me, and we do have some business to discuss. Would you consider me extremely rude if I ask you to excuse us? We will go into the next cabin for a few minutes."

"I understand, but if you need privacy I shall leave." He stood up and took her hand. "Thank you for a most enjoyable afternoon."

"Thank you, but the pleasure was equally mine." Her smile was full of hidden meaning once more and she finished, "You will call upon me again — tomorrow."

"Without fail." Mason lifted her hand and gallantly kissed it. Then he turned to Shafi and bade him goodbye.

★ ★ ★

As his *shikara* carried him to the shore he wondered why Vandana had chosen to confront him with the Pakistani. For despite her feigned embarrassment when Shafi had arrived, he was certain that she had deliberately arranged to bring them together.

10

The Enemy

That same afternoon Panjit Sangh received another visit from the Military Police. He was alone when the knock sounded on his door and he went hopefully to answer it. He was expecting a call from Shareena, but his smile quickly faded as he opened the door. He recognized the thin, weasel features of Captain Dayal Sen, the officer who had conducted all of the previous interrogations, and behind him the large, solid sergeant who had always remained silent and who had never been introduced. A constable was also present, but Sangh was mystified by the fourth man who made up the group. He was a large Sikh, magnificently bearded as all his race, and with his beard contained in a tight chin-strap hairnet. His black eyes were cold and level. Sangh returned his gaze for a moment, and was slowly conscious of some faint, psychic warning tracing patterns of danger along his spine. He sensed that this was no ordinary visit, and that today more than ever he needed to be on his guard.

Dayal Sen said politely, "Good afternoon, Lieutenant Sangh. I am afraid that we find it necessary to ask you some more questions. You will permit us to enter."

It was not a question but a statement. Sangh shifted his weight on his stick and stood aside to let them pass. No one spoke for a moment and then he preceded them into his living-room. The constable stayed by the outer door while the sergeant posted himself just inside the living-room. Sangh sat down on the divan and looked up at his unwanted guests.

"Well," he asked. "What is it now?"

Dayal Sen sat down opposite him, but the big Sikh had turned away and was casually examining the room. The Sikh was the only one who was not in army uniform, but Sangh was sure that he was superior to all the rest. He found that he had difficulty in concentrating on Sen as his interrogater said, "We are still interested in the letter that was found at the army camp on the night that a top secret filing cabinet was broken open and two sentries were murdered. That letter could only have been dropped by the intruder, and we are not satisfied with your explanation that it was stolen from your desk. We demand to know to whom that letter was sent? Who are you trying to protect?"

Sangh said wearily, "The letter was sent to no one. It was intended for an army officer in Delhi under whom I served before my discharge on medical grounds. The letter was stolen before it could be posted."

"I see." Polite disbelief. "And the contents of the letter, offering information, unspecified but of high importance. How do you explain that?"

"I had reason to believe that I had uncovered evidence of an enemy spy network here in Kashmir. I asked my officer to put me in contact with the proper authorities to receive my information."

"But if such a thing is true then I am

the proper authority. You should have come to me." Disbelief had become polite triumph. "You are a fool, Lieutenant Sangh. Why do you not admit your guilt and save us all so much trouble."

Sangh said angrily, "If you are so convinced of my guilt why don't you arrest me?"

"Because if we are kind, perhaps you will be sensible. You have a distinguished army career behind you, and fate has been unkind by making you a cripple. If you tell us the truth then all these things can perhaps be taken into consideration to make things easier for you. So far you have only offered information to an enemy, I do not believe that you have imparted it. If so perhaps you can become a hero by telling us to whom the information was offered. All we need is the name of the person to whom that letter was sent."

The questioning was following what had become a routine pattern, and Sangh knew that they were trying to grind down his resistance. The questions were always the same, and his answers were invariably received with the same polite scorn. It was repeated over and over again, occasionally with an attack from a new angle, or a trick question inserted in the hope that he would make a wrong answer. He was becoming tired of Sen's bland, toneless voice, and the thin, smugly infuriating face, and so he ignored the man's words completely. It was pointless to go back over his weak defences, and so he tried to attack.

"What have you done about the woman Vandana?" he demanded. "I am sure that she had something to do with the raid on the army camp. I informed you of my suspicions the last time you were here. Have you interrogated her yet?"

For a rare moment Dayal Sen's face became flustered. He said curtly, "I do not consider it necessary. The lady you mention is a highly respectable person. I cannot impose upon her privacy simply because you attempt to tell lies to draw attention from yourself."

"Surely you are not doing your duty if you will not even check upon my story," Sangh snapped back. "Nobody is so respectable that the police dare not make even discreet enquiries."

Dayal Sen hesitated, and then a deep, harsh voice interrupted.

"Your story has been checked, Lieutenant. I myself made the discreet enquiries you suggest, and I am satisfied that there is absolutely no truth in your foolish allegations."

Sangh looked up and stared into the cold black eyes. In the rising heat of the moment he had forgotten the silent Sikh standing in the background. The big man towered over him and his arms were calmly folded across his broad chest. They fought a long, staring battle, and it was Sangh who finally had to blink his eyes. He said angrily, "Who are you?"

Dayal Sen said promptly. "This is Major Singh."

"All Sikhs are named Singh," Sangh retorted.

"I am Major Chandra Singh," the Major said impressively.

"Military Intelligence?"

"Perhaps, but I am now in charge of this case. That is all you need to know."

159

The Sikh reached out one hand and drew up the second heavy armchair as easily as if it had been a piano stool. He sat down and delicately hitched up the trousers of his dark suit before placing his large hands upon his knees. He settled his bulky body and his black eyes bored into Sangh's face from beneath a dark blue turban. In that moment Panjit Sangh was certain that he was facing his real enemy. It was an instinctive feeling, but there was no doubt in his mind that the Major was the man who was protecting Vandana, and once more the cold snake of warning wriggled along his spine. There had to be some definite reason for Chandra Singh to come out in the open and face him, and the feeling of impending danger was strong.

The Major said flatly, "Lieutenant, you have wasted too much of Captain Sen's valuable time. All your excuses and explanations have proved to be futile lies and fabrications. Now is the time for us to start again. We will forget all that you have told Captain Sen. You will tell me the name of the person to whom you addressed that letter."

"I have already told you — "

"The truth, Lieutenant. The truth!" The bearded face thrust forward and the words were a military bark. "Perhaps you do not realize the seriousness of this affair. Two Indian soldiers have been foully murdered. Top secret papers have been examined by a hostile agent and almost certainly photographed. Those papers contained complete details of all our military defence forces in Kashmir and Ladakh. They reveal our strength and the deployment of all our troops and installations. They give a vital advantage to any enemy who wishes to make a full scale attack upon India. That is the size of the case in which you have become involved. To attempt to cover up the perpetrators of these crimes is treason of the highest order. For this you can be shot. If you have any loyalty whatever left to India then you must tell us the truth."

There was a tight, knotted anger building up inside Panjit Sangh, and he had to restrain the burning impulse to smash into the dark, bearded face with the stick he still grasped in his right hand. He looked away from the Sikh and addressed his answer to Dayal Sen.

"I have told you the truth," he repeated bitterly. "You must believe it. India's enemy is the woman Vandana."

The police captain did not answer but looked at Chandra Singh. Finally Sangh too had to turn his gaze back to the Sikh, and he knew now that the Major was fully in charge of the investigation. His position was hopeless.

He had been vaguely aware that Chandra Singh had moved while he had been facing Sen, but he was not prepared for what came next. Singh's right hand still rested palm down on his knee, but abruptly he leaned forward and raised the hand upwards. The movement was so sharp that Sangh expected a blow and flinched backwards, but the hand merely held a photograph. The question lashed at him with a note of triumph.

"This man! You have seen him before!"

Panjit Sangh recovered himself and

looked more closely at the photograph. It was of a handsome, dark-skinned man wearing a white shirt. The man was smiling and there was a neat pencil-line moustache above his upper lip. Sangh had never seen the face before and he shook his head. He looked up and saw an expression of what might have been disappointment cross the face of his enemy, as though Chandra Singh had expected his shock tactics to have some positive effect. Dayal Sen was also watching attentively.

Sangh said calmly, "I am sorry, you cannot startle me with this photograph, for the simple reason that I do not know this man."

There was silence, and then Chandra Singh took a fat wallet from inside his jacket and placed the photograph inside. His face showed nothing now, but after a moment he returned to the routine pattern of all the previous investigations.

The questioning was the most savage yet and lasted for another hour, and at the end Sangh was flustered, angry and defeated. He fully expected Chandra

Singh to finish the interview by having him removed to an army cell, and was surprised when the Major did nothing of the sort. Instead Singh reminded him that he was still under open arrest and was forbidden to leave Srinagar without military permission, and then he departed with his three aides.

Panjit Sangh watched them leave with a mixture of violent feelings, and wondered over the possible implications of the photograph.

★ ★ ★

That evening at dusk Mason paid a second furtive visit to compare notes with his old friend. He approached *Chenar Vale* by a roundabout route and arrived at the back door of the house after making his way through the darkness of the apple orchard. He was confident that the house would be under surveillance and that he would be seen entering, but he took the precautions nonetheless. Panjit Sangh admitted him into the living-room and he saw at once that his friend was disturbed.

Sangh quickly recounted the events of the afternoon and finished emphatically, "Chandra Singh is the traitor whom I suspected must exist in Indian Military Intelligence. I am sure of it. He said that he personally investigated my allegations against Vandana and found them to be groundless. And that means that he has to be the man who is protecting her."

Mason drummed his fingers reflectively on the arm of his chair, the same chair in which Chandra Singh had been seated only a few hours previously. He said slowly, "It sounds feasible. But why should Chandra Singh come out into the open? It seems a needless risk, and there must be a reason."

"Because Dayal Sen was beginning to believe my story," Sangh exclaimed. "That is the reason. Chandra Singh had to pretend to make enquiries about Vandana, otherwise Sen would have followed up my story. Sen believes I am guilty, but I think he is trying to do his job. Chandra Singh has now taken over the whole investigation so that he can cut in and stop me if I begin to convince

Sen of my innocence."

The flow of words ceased for a moment as another thought crossed Sangh's mind, and then he added, "Also I think he wanted to show me that photograph."

Mason's interest sharpened. "What photograph?"

"A picture of a man whom I have never seen before. Yet Chandra Singh showed it to me suddenly as though he expected to shock me into making some admission as though I did know him. Or perhaps — " His brow furrowed, " — perhaps that was just an act to impress Dayal Sen. I have a strange feeling about that photograph, as though it was the whole point of the interview."

Mason was leaning forward. He said slowly, "I think I can describe the man in that photograph. Check me if I'm wrong." He paused to verify his memory and then continued. "A youngish man, in his thirties. Rather athletic, good-looking. A Pakistani with a slim little moustache."

Sangh stared at him in surprise.

"A Pakistani, yes. The description fits.

That picture reminded me of something but I could not think what. But now I know. The man looked very similar to one of the Pakistani cricketers who played against India in the last test match." He was still staring. "But, Paul, how did you know?"

"Because I met him this afternoon, on board the *Shalimar*. His name is Lalshar Shafi, or at least that's the name that Vandana gave him. Apparently he owns a curio shop near the sixth bridge of the Jhelum. He gave me his business card."

Mason took the card from his pocket, looked at it for a moment, and then tapped it thoughtfully against his thumb-nail.

"It's because of Shafi that I came here tonight," he admitted. "Our meeting looked like an accident and it threw Shafi off balance. He looked very worried. Vandana put on a little act too, but I'm damned sure she deliberately arranged to bring us together. I've been wondering why, and was hoping that you might have some ideas."

Sangh shook his head.

"Until today I have never heard of this man, but — " He frowned. "Let us think about this carefully. Vandana deliberately arranges for you to encounter this Lalshar Shafi, and at the same time Chandra Singh goes to the trouble of showing me the Pakistani's photograph. Why?"

"They obviously have a reason for concentrating our interest on Shafi."

Sangh nodded. "But again why? Is he what you would call a red herring? Are they just trying to divert our interest from something or someone of real importance? Or are they baiting some kind of a trap?"

Mason said softly, "If I relied upon instinct I would scent a trap, but there is only one way in which to make sure."

"What is that?"

"To do what is obviously expected of me, follow the bait and tomorrow pay a visit to Shafi's shop."

Sangh's face was worried. He said bluntly, "And if it is a trap?"

Mason smiled wryly. "Then it's up to me to spring it, without getting caught."

11

The Trap

It was mid-morning when Mason walked into Srinagar to pay his casual call upon Lalshar Shafi, and within five minutes of leaving the Hotel Jahan he knew that he had a shadow. He reached the main bridge where the Jhelum made a sharp turn from his left to flow through the more ancient part of the city, and by then he was certain that he had two. He did not look round but turned right along the bank of the river, past the floating townships of moored houseboats.

Outwardly he was relaxed but his brain was working hard. He had expected to be followed but two shadows seemed an unnecessary risk. Also they were staying very close to his heels, as though it were vital that they should not lose him, regardless of whether they were identified. The situation nagged at his mind and there were two possible answers. One was that he had convinced Vandana that he was nothing more than a clumsy amateur, which would mean that his shadows had no respect for him and were becoming careless. The other was that Vandana had seen through the double game that he was trying to play, and was confident that he would continue to play the amateur, pretend that he had not noticed the two men behind, and still visit Shafi as was expected of him. They were still playing at double-thinking, the endless game of mental chess with themselves as the major pieces which eventually had to move. And whichever way he looked at it, he was now certain that he was walking into a trap.

He had to turn away from the river, passing through a shanty town of old wooden houses and tiny open shops. The shops all seemed to be occupied by tailors, squatting on their heels behind their sewing machines and gossiping with their customers. He crossed over a canal and there were more picturesque views of the moored houseboats along the river, on many of them the slanting roofs were gaily sprinkled with carpets of red peppers drying in the sun. In the open the sunshine was warm, but in the narrower streets the air was damper and darker. Here there were swarms of people, dark-faced little Kashmiris with their shirt tails flapping outside of baggy trousers, and shuffling women muffled in long shawls that were pulled over their heads. Mason's two shadows had dropped well back along the river bank, but now they again closed up behind him.

They were both Indians, a little taller than the average Kashmiris, and without the cheerful smiles with which most of the passing crowds were inflicted. He was sure that they were at least semi-professional, for they were using most of the familiar tricks. They were inter-changing very smoothly so that it was not always the same one who was directly behind. If they had not been pressing him so close Mason might have had difficulty in finding them. It was not their presence but their confidence that began to worry him.

He had three alternatives. One was to ascertain Vandana's intentions by calmly walking into the prepared trap, and trusting in his own abilities to get himself out of it again. Two was to lose his two shadows, make a more professional reconnoitre of Shafi's business premises and only approach the Pakistani if it were safe. And three was to call off the whole thing, lead his two shadows round and round in ever decreasing circles, and finally go home.

The last was negative, without risk but without gain, and he dismissed it automatically. The second alternative he considered but finally he discarded that also. He knew that he was capable of losing his two shadows if he wished, but there was no relative value in the move. He was certain that Shafi's shop would be watched, just as he was certain that *Chenar Vale* and his own hotel had also been kept under continuous observation, and so an advance reconnoitre would tell him nothing. He would merely be faced again with the decision to either spring

172

the trap or call off the whole thing. To make any progress at all he had to take the risk of entering the trap.

He reached the sixth bridge of the Jhelum, and halted on the bridge itself. There were attractive views in both directions. Up river was the pointed silver roof of a temple, then the rickety wooden structure of the fifth bridge, and beyond a distant glimpse of a pagoda spire of the largest of the riverside temples. The sun was warm, and the river was a winding ribbon of silver-blue. Mason brought Shafi's business card out of his pocket and re-read the address.

He was uncertain of his way, and for a moment he was tempted to turn back and blandly ask directions from one of the two men who had been glued to his heels. The imp of humour had to be suppressed, and somewhat reluctantly he showed the card to a passing youth who had halted on his bicycle. The youth examined the card, jabbered with some companions who had skidded up beside him, and then they all decided that Mason should go back the way he had come and turn left. Mason thanked them and went in the direction they had pointed out. He was careful not to notice his two shadows who were busily purchasing some sweetcakes from a street vendor who had parked his barrow on the opposite side of the road.

He found the shop two minutes later. It was an unimpressive wooden building bearing a sign with the words *Kashmir Art and Curio Emporium*. The frontage was shabby and there was very little paint on the old wooden boards. A tiny, nagging voice of doubt told him that this was his last chance to turn around and walk away, but instead Mason climbed up the small flight of three wooden steps that led up to the shop doorway. His two shadows had not reappeared, the street was almost empty, and the normal babble of noise had hushed. All his senses were alert but there was nothing to alarm him. He knocked on the door and went inside.

He was in a large, gloomy room, where the myriad specks of dust floated clearly in the few rays of sunlight that penetrated through the windows. All around him were shelves filled with wood carvings, fruit bowls, polished animals, weird Hindu deities, face masks and wall plaques. It was similar to the shop that he had inspected on his first day in Srinagar, except that here there was a large variety of articles other than in wood. There were jewel boxes in colourful papier mache, a range of curios in ivory and jade, and a large selection of heavy silver jewellery.

Mason glanced round slowly, and then a shuffling sound brought his attention to an old man who was moving to meet him from one of the darkened corners. He wore a brightly-patterned skull cap and an old brown jacket that was far too long for him, and when he smiled Mason counted exactly four teeth along his lower gum. There was no one else in the shop.

For the next few minutes Mason looked and listened attentively as the old man showed him various pieces and quoted their prices. He handled some of the carvings, agreeing that the wood was beautifully polished, and at the same time marked down the exits from the shop. There was only the front door, and a smaller door at the back. The windows were almost wholly blocked by shelves and could be ruled out. Finally he asked, "Is Mister Shafi here?"

The old man hesitated and Mason looked up from an elegant piece of ivory which he had brought over to the light. He went on casually.

"That's Mister Lalshar Shafi. I met him yesterday and he said that he might be able to show me some more unusual pieces."

The old man stared for another few moments, and then he nodded.

"Upstairs," he said. "I show you."

Mason replaced the ivory carving and followed the old man over to the small door at the back end of the shop. They went through, and in the room beyond two men were squatting among piles of shavings and working hard on more carvings. They exchanged smiles but said nothing, and Mason's guide led him up a flight of bare wooden steps to the second floor. There was a dark landing with a door on either side. The old man gestured to Mason to wait, and then knocked on the nearer door. A voice from inside bade him enter and he opened the door and went in. There was an exchange of words and then Shafi appeared in the doorway. He wore white trousers and a white shirt, but he did not smile. His whole body was tense.

Mason stepped forward, smiling calmly as he offered his hand.

"Hello. You gave me your card, remember. I thought I'd take you up on that offer of cheap souvenirs."

Shafi shook hands briefly and then invited him inside. The Pakistani was controlling himself well, but Mason could sense his concealed agitation. Shafi was as shaken by his presence here as he had been by their meeting on the *Shalimar*. Mason had the feeling that the Pakistani was living on his nerves, and suddenly he was sure that the man had no conscious part in the plot that was evolving around them. Whatever Vandana had planned Shafi

177

was not a conspiring participant. It was more likely that he was merely another unsuspecting victim. Mason's inbuilt warning system began hitting all signals and he knew that he too was becoming over-tense. Shafi's reaction had underlined his conviction that he was in some kind of a trap, and he had the feeling that at any second the jaws would snap.

Shafi dismissed his assistant, and while the old man was taking his leave Mason had a moment to inspect the room. It was a business office, littered with account books and ledgers. There was a large desk and a big filing cabinet. The walls were papered brown and the only relief was a large calendar with a coloured picture of Naga dancers from Assam. Behind the desk was a closed window, and Mason noted that it looked down over the street. The door closed behind the old man and then Shafi moved behind his desk and sat down. He pulled open the top drawer, hesitated, and then looked squarely at Mason.

"Who are you? What do you want?"

Mason smiled. "I thought you remembered. My name is Paul Mason. I'm a friend of Vandana's. We met yesterday at her houseboat, and you invited me to call here. You promised that you could offer me good prices on some wood carvings."

Shafi stared at him uncertainly, and then he kicked back his chair and stood up. He went to the window, and for a moment he looked down into the street. Then he said bluntly, "You were followed."

Mason looked suitably alarmed and quickly moved to join the Pakistani at the window. He studied the scene below and immediately spotted the two men who had followed him from his hotel. They were standing on the far side of the road, and were watching the door of the curio shop which was directly below. There were other people in the street and Mason knew that Shafi was coldly watching his face. He allowed his expression to reflect confusion and asked uncertainly, "Who by? Where?"

As he spoke an army jeep appeared and

pulled up with a fast screech of brakes. A second jeep appeared behind it and four military policemen scrambled out even before it had stopped. Mason's two shadows were hurrying into the centre of the road, and a burly Sikh in an army uniform with the rank tabs of a major was climbing swiftly out of the first jeep. Mason's warning system abruptly stopped because now it was too late, and he felt icy cold. The big Sikh looked upwards as he issued sharp orders, but Mason did not need the brief glimpse of the black eyes beneath the blue turban, and the black-bearded face with its tight little chin-strap hairnet. He had already guessed that this could only be Major Chandra Singh.

It no longer mattered what kind of a face he showed to Lalshar Shafi, for they were both caught in the same snare. Mason saw too late that he had not been followed by hirelings of Vandana as he had supposed, but by agents of Chandra Singh's Military Intelligence, and now the whole plot tumbled neatly into place.

Shafi had been spying for Pakistan,

perhaps through Vandana, or perhaps Vandana had only approached him when she saw how he could be made to fit into her plans. The details were unimportant. The facts were that the net around Shafi was ready to close, and Chandra Singh had only waited until Mason had been neatly manoeuvred into the same net. If they were taken together then Mason would be incriminated with the Pakistani spy ring, which in turn would incriminate Panjit Sangh and complete the case that had been built up against him. The way would be open for Vandana to continue her spying activities for the Chinese.

The finished picture ran swiftly through Mason's mind, and his face became hard. He had overplayed the clumsy amateur and now the trap was sprung with a vengeance. His only course now was to get out fast and his only hope was to work together with Shafi. He turned quickly with an apology on his lips and then froze.

Shafi had moved back to his desk and from the open drawer he had quietly lifted a heavy black Luger. The Pakistani's dark face was a bitter mask, and the gun was pointed at Mason's heart. He said coldly, "You brought them here. Now give me one good reason why I should not kill you."

* * *

At that same time Panjit Sangh was alone at his home. He had started to work on a new chapter of his book, but after he had torn out and balled up the third consecutive sheet of paper from his typewriter he had to admit that he was incapable of concentration. He had tried to write as an alternative to worrying over the possible results of Mason's visit to Lalshar Shafi, but it was of no use. He sat back from his desk and for the thousandth time he cursed the stiff and twisted right leg that prevented him from fighting his own battles. It galled him to merely sit there doing nothing while Mason was taking all the risks on his behalf.

He had spent an almost sleepless night in trying to reason out Vandana's intentions, but he had arrived at no conclusions. They were a trap, but what kind of a trap. Mason was confident that he could spring the trap and then turn events to his own advantage, but Sangh was not so sure. He had faith in Mason, but he also had a more revealing knowledge of Vandana. He had failed, and failed miserably in his own attempts to defeat her in the subtle game of mental manoeuvres, and he was pessimistic toward's Mason's chances of success. He had a premonition that things could go badly and horribly wrong.

He reached for the cup of coffee that he had made some fifteen minutes previously, but the coffee had become cold. He pulled a wry face as he sipped it and decided that he might as well make a fresh cup. He needed something to do while he waited.

He started to get up, but in that same moment he heard a faint sound behind him. He turned his head and saw the back door slowly opening. He became still, and then just as slowly lowered the cup of cold coffee to his desk. His right hand drew away from the saucer and dropped to the handle of the desk drawer.

The back door opened and a man stepped inside. He wore a black turban, black trousers and a black shirt. His shoes were soft slippers and made no sound. His face was thin with deep hollow eyes, and Sangh automatically remembered Shareena's description of the man who had followed her to New Delhi. The face was starved. The mark of Shiva was upon his forehead and he gripped a long scarf of black silk in his two hands.

The two moved simultaneously. The intruder sprang forward and Sangh yanked hard on the desk drawer. He twisted round on his seat as the drawer came open and then he grabbed up the heavy army revolver that lay just inside. He brought it up level but before he could curl his finger round the trigger the scarf struck. With the speed of a striking viper the ribbon of silk flashed forward, and the coin weight curled it around Sangh's wrist. The scarf snapped like a whip and

Sangh's wrist was almost broken as the revolver went tumbling from his fingers.

For a second they stared at each other, and then the man with the hollowed eyes began to grin. It was a death's head grin, a skull clothed only with dark brown skin.

Sangh reached for his stick, twisting backwards to snatch with his left hand. He was on his feet now but his balance was unsteady and his stiff leg slowed his movements. He found the stick but before he could bring it round to defend himself another ribbon of black silk floated down almost gently before his eyes. It dropped around his throat and was tightened from behind. He was dragged backward and only checked by the bony knee that was thrusting into the base of his spine. His right hand was still held by the first scarf and he dropped his stick as he tried to claw at the strangling hold around his neck with the fingers of his left hand. His head was bursting and his senses sinking into blackness through a dizzy red mist. The death's head was still grinning, grinning, grinning, until mercifully it dissolved into darkness.

Zakir and Kalam exchanged satisfied glances as the young lieutenant slumped between them, and then retrieved their strangling scarves as his body crumpled to the floor.

12

Escape into the Jhelum

Mason did not look down at the Luger, instead he gazed straight into Shafi's dark eyes. He said flatly, "I can give you three good reasons. One, the shot will bring them direct to this room. Two, you cannot afford to waste the time. And three, it's not necessary. And even in our business an unnecessary killing is a mistake."

Shafi hesitated and Mason went on swiftly.

"Don't you understand? I didn't lead them here. They were ready to close in on you anyway. They only waited to catch me in the same net."

"You mentioned *our* business. On which side are you? Where do you fit into — "

There was a crashing sound from below, probably as the shop door was smashed open, and the Pakistani looked round sharply. Mason could have jumped him but he knew that there was no need to take the risk. There was a startled yell from the old man who tended the shop, and then muffled shouts from the workers in the back room. A dominating voice roared orders but the general uproar denoted confusion. Shafi made up his mind abruptly and slapped the Luger down on the desk. He heaved at one corner of the heavy piece of furniture and said desperately, "Help me! We must barricade the door."

Mason grabbed the other side of the desk and together they rushed it across the floor and jammed it solidly across the doorway. Shafi ran back to the filing cabinet, twisted it round and leaned it back against the desk. Mason moved to the window and slammed it open, then he looked back for the Pakistani. He said grimly, "They've left two soldiers with rifles to watch the street. Cover me while I swing up on to the roof, and then I'll pull you up behind me."

Shafi shook his head. He had yanked

open one of the drawers of the filing cabinet and was pulling out a fistful of papers.

"No. I must burn these."

"Then you can't escape. Give me the gun."

"No." Shafi dropped the papers to the floor and snatched up the Luger. For the second time it pointed at Mason's heart.

"I'm sorry, Mister Mason. But I need the gun to hold them off while I reduce these papers to ashes. Escape if you can, but I cannot help you."

Mason hesitated for a second, and then they both heard the rush of footsteps pounding up the stairs. A barrage of fists crashed upon the door and the barking voice of Chandra Singh demanded that it be opened. Shafi watched Mason, but with his left hand he reached into the filing cabinet and drew out a bottle. He extracted the cork with his teeth and poured paraffin over the papers at his feet. He said softly, "Thank you for helping me to barricade the door, but now it is each man for himself. I must

189

finish my job, you must escape. I hope you succeed. I do not understand your presence here, but I feel that it cannot be beneficial to either of us to be caught together."

As he spoke Shafi had produced a cigarette lighter with his left hand. He snapped it into flame and knelt to fire the heap of soaked papers at his feet. As they blazed he heaped more papers on top from the filing cabinet. From outside there was the combined sound of heavy shoulders attacking the door, and Shafi calmly sent a bullet from the Luger crashing through the woodwork. There was a yell of pain and flustered shouts, and the sound of a hasty retreat.

Mason went back to the window and looked down. The two Indian soldiers were standing by the second jeep, their rifles unslung from their shoulders and ready in their hands. To climb out of the window was asking for a bullet in the back, but there was no other exit. He needed the Luger to cover himself, but he knew he could expect no help from Shafi. The Pakistani had his own problems. Mason drew a deep breath, and then without a backward glance he scrambled fast out of the window.

The two soldiers were watching the door of the shop as Mason stepped up on to the window sill. He leaned out over the street, lunged one hand upwards and caught at the projecting overhang of the roof. There was no time to test whether the ancient wood was capable of holding his weight and with a prayer he snatched a second hold and hauled himself up. The move was smoothly executed in a minimum of time, and he was wriggling his belly on to the gentle slope of the roof when a shout from below told him that the alarm had been raised. A rifle cracked and Mason rolled forward and to his left, and in the same moment he heard a fresh outbreak of violence from the room he had just left as Lalshar Shafi exchanged a sudden fusilade of shots with Chandra Singh and his men on the upstairs landing.

Mason's rolling movement carried him further on to the roof as the rifle bullet ricocheted off the wall where his legs had dangled a moment before, but as his momentum stopped he began to slither helplessly back towards the edge. He clawed at the tiles and then one of them broke free and slipped behind him to crash into the street, and then he dug his fingers into the hole he had made. He pulled himself to his feet with another desperate scrambling movement, ran three quick strides and dived flat again as the two rifles cracked viciously behind him. The bullets passed over his head as his outflung hands fastened on the apex of the roof and he hauled his body forward, rolling over the top and tumbling down the far slope as more shooting shattered the tiles behind him. He hung on with one hand to check his fall, and then released his grip and slithered slowly to the far edge. He was out of sight and out of range, but he was sweating and his heart was pumping furiously. If his first hold had broken and he had fallen back . . . if he had not moved with such suicide speed . . . if the two soldiers had been less flustered and more accurate . . . There were so many ifs that could have cost him his life, and even now there was no time to stop and think.

He balanced precariously on the very edge of the roof and saw that from this side he was looking down on the Jhelum. Directly below him was a balcony that overhung the river, and he swung himself down towards it. Behind him there was still the violent sound of shooting coming from inside the building, and he could picture Shafi crouching behind the protective shield of the filing cabinet and desk and holding off the irate Indians with his Luger while he completed the task of burning his papers. Mason earnestly wished the Pakistani the very best of luck, for while Shafi was keeping Chandra Singh occupied, his own chances of escape were increased.

He dropped on to the balcony, and at the same time a Sikh soldier gripping a rifle stepped out from a concealed door to face him. The man had clearly been sent to cover the back of the house but he was seconds too late. Mason knocked the rifle barrel aside with a sweep of his arm and his right fist crashed forward to slam against the bearded jaw and send the man toppling down. Then Mason stepped on to the balcony and took a long, sloping dive into the cold, silver waters of the Jhelum.

The icy shock almost stopped his heart as he plunged deep, but he stayed down and swam hard under the surface. He had filled his lungs with air during the dive and he was an excellent swimmer. In fact, his initial transfer from the Royal Marines to Naval Intelligence had been made when Allan Kendall had needed a first rate man for a particularly dangerous mission entailing underwater sabotage. Now he felt almost at home, and had no difficulty in reaching the far side of the river before he came up for air.

He surfaced beside a long raft of floating logs that lay close against the far bank, and dragged himself out of the water. Many of the logs were loose and rolling beneath him, and as he lay across them he heard shouting voices and another shot from a rifle. He looked upstream and saw that he was only a matter of sixty yards from the nearest bridge where two more Sikh soldiers were calling on him to halt. Mason swore as he scrambled upright and fought for a moment to regain his balance, then he began to run fast along the floating logs. They shifted dangerously beneath his feet but he moved with his arms spread wide, leaving the logs spinning in his wake but staying as sure-footed as a Canadian lumberjack.

The soldiers on the bridge hesitated, and then decided that it was a waste of time to keep shooting at his wildly moving body. Instead they hurried across the bridge to try and circle down to the riverside and give chase. Along this side of the river the ancient buildings were built right down to the water's edge, and there were no alleys through which Mason could make his escape. The raft of logs came to an end and without hesitation Mason dived back into the river. An excited crowd had now gathered on the bridge and were shouting advice to the two soldiers who had reappeared from a flight of steps that sloped down the water's edge, but again Mason stayed under and swam for his life.

He recrossed the Jhelum and surfaced quietly by the hull of a moored houseboat. He regained his breath, and while he was momentarily hidden he paused to survey the situation. The two soldiers were moving gingerly along the raft of logs but in grave danger of falling between them. The crowd on the bridge was still shouting advice, but none of them seemed to realize that the quarry was no longer on their side of the river. Mason smiled briefly and then looked along his own side of the Jhelum.

He was perhaps fifty yards below the balcony from which he had made his first dive, and now he could see the dark blue turban that belonged to Chandra Singh leaning out as the Major bawled at the two soldiers on the logs. There was no more shooting from inside the building and Mason realized grimly that Lalshar Shafi had either been taken or killed. He drew a deep breath, and then submerged and swam another thirty yards downriver to reach the shelter of another houseboat.

When he came up again he was well clear of all the activity that was taking place below the bridge. The houseboat that provided his shield appeared to be deserted, and after listening for a moment to ensure himself on this point he swam behind the boat to the bank. Here again the ancient wooden buildings reached to the water's edge and he had to swim along beside them until he came to a sloping stone ramp leading down from an alley that connected the river with the nearest street. It was impossible to climb out without smearing himself with the filthy black mud that was plastered along the edge of the ramp, and he emerged dripping and with his clothes badly soiled. He tore the silk cravat from his throat and used it to wipe off the worst of the mud as he hurried away.

He had entered the trap and escaped it, but he had gained no advantage and his present position was far from satisfactory. And so far he had definitely come off second best.

★ ★ ★

There was only one course of action now, and that was to fall back on the instinct of past experience. He knew that it would be dangerous to go direct to Panjit Sangh, but he also knew that Vandana would leave no loose ends to her well-laid plans, and his intuition told him that the young Lieutenant was in danger. Despite the risk that it involved for himself Mason headed for *Chenar Vale*.

He used the back alleys to make a wide circle round the area of the sixth bridge, and hoped that Chandra Singh would be delayed by the fruitless search that his men were now making along the far river bank, and in clearing up the mess that would remain after the battle with Shafi. The Sikh Major would eventually realize that his second quarry had slipped past him and then he too would hurry to *Chenar Vale*, but Mason considered it reasonable to hope that a little time would elapse before that happened.

Startled faces watched him pass but no one tried to hinder his progress, and he regained the crowded main streets opposite the fourth of the nine bridges that spanned the Jhelum. He pushed his way through the crowds and then spotted a bicycle leaning against the wall. It was exactly what he needed, for in this area a bicycle would be faster than a car. The owner did not appear to be watching and so Mason straddled the machine and quickly pedalled off. It was done so swiftly that there was not even an outcry behind him.

For the next ten minutes he hurtled crazily through the narrow, jostling streets, ringing madly at the little bell on the handlebars and yelling lustily to clear his path. Mercifully the brakes were good and he had to apply them fast time and time again to avoid head-on collisions with pedestrians and other cyclists, and once he was only just successful in skidding past a horse-drawn tonga that all but sandwiched him against a wall. He left a wake of cursing, indignant citizens but did not once look back.

His clothes were uncomfortably cold and wet, but the exertion of pedalling kept him from shivering. The cycle bounced and rattled noisily beneath him and one unexpected crack in the road surface almost threw him off. The saddle was hard and painful, and he was thankful when he swung out of the old part of Srinagar and leaned the cycle round a racing curve into the wide road that slashed through the more modern part of the city. Here there was a flurry of motor traffic, and he dumped the cycle on the pavement in order to wave down a passing taxi.

He ran to pull open the back door as the taxi drew to a stop and scrambled inside. The driver twisted round from the wheel, saw the wet, bedraggled state of his passenger and began to protest. Mason shut him up, showed a wallet full of soggy notes, and curtly told him to drive on.

It took another fifteen minutes to drive out to *Chenar Vale*. Mason paid the driver handsomely, despite the difficulty of peeling the notes apart, and then told him to wait. He got out on to the road, hesitated as he glanced around the gardens and orchards that surrounded the large wooden house, and then pushed open the gate and hurried up the path.

The front door opened while he was still three yards away, and for one horrible, sinking moment he thought that Chandra Singh had arrived here ahead of him. Then he saw that it was not one of his enemies who awaited him, and neither was it Panjit Sangh. Instead Shareena ran almost hysterically into his arms.

The Indian girl was so distraught that he could get no sense out of her, and so he hustled her inside. They entered the kitchen and immediately he saw the cause of her distress. From the centre beam of the ceiling a knotted rope had been fixed, and its lower end was looped into an ugly hangman's noose. The kitchen table had been pushed back out of the way, and huddled in a limp heap below the noose was the still body of Panjit Sangh.

Mason's face became hard, but his hands were gentle as he pushed Shareena to one side. He knelt beside Sangh and then relief flooded through him as he saw that the young Indian was alive. There were bluish bruise marks on the side of his neck, but he was still breathing.

Mason glanced up at the girl.

"How did you find him?"

"Just — just as he is now." She had to swallow hard and went on. "I knocked on the door, and heard some scuffling sounds inside. There was no answer and so I opened the door and saw — and saw Panjit lying there beneath that awful rope. I thought he was dead. I thought — "

"How long ago?"

"About ten minutes. I tried to revive him, and then I heard your car driving up."

Mason looked through into the living-room. Both doors were standing open and he could see through to the apple orchard beyond. He said flatly, "Someone was trying to arrange a suicide. Your arrival must have frightened them off."

His face was bleak and he knew that his instinct had been right to bring him here. Vandana and Chandra Singh had indeed arranged to tie up all the loose ends, and the last details of their plans were fitting neatly into place. The suicide scene would have been the final touch after rounding up Lalshar Shafi and collecting evidence of the Pakistani's spying activities. What would be more logical than that Shafi should telephone a warning to his accomplice as the police closed in, and that the accomplice should despair and take his own life. The last link would be forged, and with Sangh dead his guilt would be accepted.

The young Indian was beginning to stir and Shareena brought a wet cloth to speed his recovery. Now that Mason had arrived the girl was steadier, and although her hands still trembled her panic had disappeared. Between them they brought Sangh back to consciousness and then helped him to sit up. His eyes were dazed when the first flickered open, and then they cleared and reflected horror as he saw the waiting noose suspended above his head. He succumbed to a fit of hoarse coughing and only then was he able to talk.

His story was brief. He could only repeat Shareena's description of the man with the starved face, and add that a second strangler had attacked him from behind. That was all he knew.

Mason said grimly, "I'd lay odds that they were Vandana's two servants. The man you didn't see was probably Zakir. They didn't kill you outright because they wanted you to be found dangling from this rope. They were setting the scene when Shareena interrupted them, and fortunately for both of you they didn't stop to realize that she was just a girl on her own. They simply took to their heels and bolted through the back of the house."

Sangh nodded weakly, and then he noticed the state of Mason's clothing. He said anxiously, "Paul, what has been happening to you?"

Mason explained as briefly as he could. He finished, "The case against you is sewn up pretty neatly. There's no doubt that Chandra Singh's Intelligence agents can produce eye-witness accounts of my visits here to you. This morning two of his agents followed me to Shafi's shop. Two so that each could corroborate the other's report in a military court. The link between you and myself, and then myself and Shafi was positively established, and

204

so then the trap was sprung. You were to be found dead so that it would look as though either Shafi or I had telephoned a warning that had panicked you into suicide."

Sangh said bitterly, "I believe it. Vandana is devilish enough to have planned everything as you say."

Shareena had listened closely, trying to understand, and now she asked wretchedly, "But what can we do now? What will happen next?"

"What will happen is that Chandra Singh is probably on his way here now, ostensibly to make an arrest but in reality expecting to find a body." Mason looked at Sangh and went on quietly. "I'm sorry, Lieutenant, but the only thing you can do now is to stay here and wait to be arrested. If you tried to get away you wouldn't get far with that crippled leg, and the attempt would only be taken as proving your guilt when what we want is to prove your innocence."

Sangh nodded slowly but Shareena tried to protest. Mason cut her short and went on swiftly, "You'll have to stay here too. Stick close beside Panjit as much as you can, because while the two of you are together you'll give Chandra Singh no chance to stage a second suicide or an accident. Now the odds are that he'll bring that Military Police Captain with him — "

"Dayal Sen," Sangh put in helpfully.

"That's right. He'll bring Sen because he'll want a reliable witness to the suicide scene he expects to find. Between you you'll have to try and convince Sen of the truth. Don't accuse Chandra Singh directly, because Sen will certainly reject that outright. If you can use the evidence of this hangman's rope and just sow a few beneficial doubts in Dayal Sen's mind then we may be getting somewhere."

Panjit Sangh nodded again, and with their combined help he struggled to his feet.

"I understand, Paul," he said weakly. "But what do you intend to do? You are in almost as much trouble as myself."

Mason smiled bleakly. "I'm going to pay a visit to the *Shalimar*. There was no telephone on the houseboat, so unless

Chandra Singh has sent a messenger to let her know what has happened, Vandana is probably under the happy delusion that I am under arrest. My appearance should prove a surprise."

He turned to go and then Sangh called, "Wait, Paul!"

Mason looked back and watched as Sangh limped through the open door into the living-room. The young Indian located his stick and the army revolver that he had been forced to drop when he had been attacked, and then he returned to the kitchen. He moved more surely with the stick to aid him and held out the gun.

"Take this, Paul. It will be of no use to me, and you might need it. Remember that Vandana's servants are killers."

Mason hesitated, and then accepted the gun.

"Thanks, Lieutenant. The time for playing games is over, and I just might decide to use it."

13

A Clue North

Mason hurried back to his taxi and told the waiting driver to take him down to the Dal Lake. During the short drive he stayed alert for any sign of Chandra Singh's military convoy racing towards *Chenar Vale*, but there was nothing to alarm him. The oncoming traffic was nothing more threatening than a few private cars, and one horse-drawn tonga trotting slowly along in the shade of the giant, red-leaved maple trees that lined the road. The taxi turned right past the great, wood-covered bulk of the Sankaracharya hill, the road following a placid waterway filled with ramshackle houseboats, which ultimately led into the lake.

As soon as he glimpsed the lake itself Mason ordered his driver to stop. He paid the man and dismissed him, and then continued on foot along the lakeside road. Here the lake was a long and narrow, inland-pointing finger with the luxury houseboats moored on the opposite side. Several hopeful Kashmiri gondoliers offered him their *shikaras*, but only one could be lucky. Mason climbed into the nearest boat and ordered the boatman to pole him out to the *Shalimar*.

So far he was not quite sure of what he intended to do, except to confront Vandana and somehow wring the truth out of her. Somewhere aboard the houseboat there had to be some kind of evidence of her own spying activities, and Mason was relying on his training and his past experience to help him find it. The heavy army revolver that Panjit Sangh had given him was thrust into the top of his trousers and hidden as much as possible beneath his grey shirt. It was large and clumsy, digging into his belly and his groin, but he was pleased to have it. He meant to make a forced search of the *Shalimar* and if Zakir and Kalam were present the gun would be needed.

It was now a little after noon, the

warmest part of the day, and with the beautiful setting of the lake to remind him Mason's thoughts strayed back to the previous afternoon when he and Vandana had lingered on their tiny island on the edge of the floating gardens. It was barely twenty-four hours since they had passionately played at love, and now he meant to face her openly as an enemy. For a moment his conscience was troubled, but then he coldly crushed it down. An Intelligence man could not afford the luxury of a conscience, and he also had to remember that she had most certainly been planning his downfall even as she had welcomed him in her arms. The love-making had been a calculated insurance, to soften him if her plans should go wrong, as they were going wrong now. There at least she could not succeed.

He expected to be seen as the *shikara* approached the *Shalimar* but no one appeared on the houseboat's decks. Slowly the *shikara* drifted over the last few yards of pure blue water, and Mason carefully peeled some more damp notes from out of his wallet and dropped them on the cushioned seat for the boatman. He told the man to wait, and when they bumped against the white hull he went aboard fast. As he reached the deck he pulled the revolver from inside his wrinkled shirt and took two swift steps to the cabin door. It was locked.

He was wary of another trap, and slowly he circled the decks. There were two more doors, both locked, and the window curtains had all been drawn so that he could not see inside. To all outward appearances the *Shalimar* was deserted and abandoned.

After making the complete circle Mason stood for a moment, listening, but there was no sound. No one had paid him any attention from the neighbouring houseboats on either side, and so he finally returned to one of the windows. The fastening was just a simple catch, and after two minutes he was able to force the window with the blade of a small clasp knife. He returned the knife to his pocket, drew the window open and parted the curtains with the barrel of the revolver. There was no alarm and so he pushed the curtain right back to admit some light into the darkened cabin. It was the same cabin in which Vandana had served him with tea and sweetcakes, but now it was bare except for the heavier furniture. Small dust covers had been draped across the tables and the divan.

Mason entered cautiously, climbing through the window and looking round. He crossed to the door that led towards the inner cabins and found that it opened easily. There was a narrow passageway that ran for the remaining length of the houseboat. On the left were two covered windows and a locked door that looked out on to the deck, and on the right the doors to four more cabins. Mason tried all the cabin doors in turn and found them open. The first cabin was clearly Vandana's bedroom, the second a dining-room, and the last two consisted of the servants' room and a kitchen. All were empty. There was no one aboard the *Shalimar*.

Mason looked down at the revolver in his hand and smiled wryly. Then he returned to the main cabin and began a more detailed search. He found that though the houseboat looked bare very little had in fact been removed. Instead everything had been carefully packed away or covered up. The job had been done tidily with no signs of hurry, and all the signs indicated a long absence but an eventual return by the occupants. He recalled Vandana saying that she normally spent the winter season in New Delhi to escape the cold, and wondered whether she had gone south.

He sat down on her bed to think the matter over, and finally he decided against it. She had been working here for several months, and he doubted that she had been working alone. It was more likely that she had been the centre-point of a small network of scattered agents, co-ordinating their reports and gradually building up an overall picture of the military defences of Kashmir. Her employers would have wanted that picture from every angle, economical, political, and most important of all full details of road conditions, accessible passes and the safest routes for bringing an attacking army over the Himalayas. Such a wealth of information could not be communicated solely by radio reports, for to be sure of their validity the Chinese would want those reports confirmed personally. The Chinese were suspicious paymasters, and the odds were that now that her task was completed Vandana had been called to face a cross-examination by high ranking intelligence officers of the Red army. The question was where?

All this was conjecture, based solely upon established espionage patterns and his own knowledge of Vandana's capabilities, but Mason was sure that he was thinking along the right lines. If he was right then he reasoned that there should be a high-powered radio transmitter hidden somewhere aboard the houseboat, and so he began to look for it. He didn't find it, but after twenty minutes he had located the place where it had been installed. There was a large, hollow cavity below the deckboards in the kitchen, and drilled holes showed where the wires had been led to connect with the electricity supply. He guessed that the transmitter itself was now somewhere on the bottom of the lake, dumped under the cover of darkness during the previous night.

He went back to the bedroom and sat down again. The fact that there had been a radio had confirmed his line of reasoning and he was now sure that Vandana had left to make a personal report to her Chinese employers. But would the interview take place in India, or would she attempt to enter China? The latter seemed improbable, for she would have to cross the icy barrier of the Himalayas, and so his thoughts turned full circle and came back to her previous trips to New Delhi. Was it possible that she made her reports to the Chinese Embassy?

The puzzle was suddenly banished from his mind as he heard a footstep on the outer deck. He picked up the revolver again and moved silently into the passage. Gently he pushed the window curtain an inch to one side, but the deck was deserted. He felt sure that the sound had not been in his imagination, and then he saw that there were now two *shikaras* waiting where there had only been his own. The upper part of the canopy was just visible on either boat. He could faintly hear the two boatmen conversing and a frown darkened his face.

He moved towards the main cabin, and then stopped as he heard a movement inside. The sound told him that someone had used his own method of entry and climbed through the window. He stepped back into the bedroom again and waited. The revolver was cocked in his hand, and yet he was more mystified than alarmed. He was sure that Vandana and her two servants had fled. Lalshar Shafi was either dead or a prisoner of the Indian Military Police, and if the visitor had been Chandra Singh then he would be backed by a heavy force of subordinates. He did not know who to expect.

He heard muffled movements from the main cabin, then uncertain steps in the passage outside. There was a moment of soft, nervous breathing, and then a slight figure in a blue sari appeared in the bedroom doorway. Mason lowered his revolver and said, "Shareena, don't move about so furtively. I might have shot you by mistake."

The girl jumped and twisted round to face him. He saw the tear stains down her cheeks and quickly went towards her. She trembled as he took her arm and said miserably, "Paul, they've taken Panjit away. The police came and — "

"All right," he said quietly. "Sit down here and take it easy. Relax and then tell me."

She sat on the bed as he directed and he seated himself beside her. The revolver he laid out of sight and then he told her to continue.

"The police came," she explained. "They placed Panjit under arrest and took him away to the army camp. I wanted to stay with him as you said, but they wouldn't let me. I couldn't do anything alone so I came to find you."

Mason's face became grim, but he offered her no rebuke. Instead he told her to wait quietly while he checked whether she had been followed. He took the revolver and went out on to the deck of the houseboat, but the encircling lake was placid and empty and he was able to breathe a sigh of relief. Chandra Singh had obviously not realized that the girl would know where to find him, and so he had not thought it worthwhile to shadow her movements. Mason was thankful for that small mercy and returned to the girl.

"Paul, I am sorry," she said wretchedly. "I didn't realize that I might be — "

"It's all right, you were not followed." He smiled to prove that he was not angry and then said, "Tell me exactly what happened when they came to arrest Panjit Sangh. I want to know everything that was said."

Shareena said slowly, "It was the big Sikh who did most of the talking. He arrived with a party of policemen, and said that he now had evidence that Panjit had been conspiring with Lalshar Shafi to pass important military secrets to Pakistan. He said that he had found photostat copies of the documents that were photographed at the army camp on the night that the two sentries were murdered and Panjit's letter was found. He said that these photostats were in a desk drawer in Shafi's office, and that they were the final proof he needed. He also added that his men had kept a check on your movements, and that he knew you were what he called a courier between Panjit and the Pakistani."

Mason said bleakly, "The whole mess is worse than I thought. Shafi was making a bonfire of his papers when I left, that was why he stayed behind, and if he did have those photostats then they were obviously the kind of thing he would have burned first. He wouldn't have made the mistake of leaving them for Chandra Singh to find. That means that Singh probably planted them himself while he searched the premises." He paused for a moment, and then asked. "Did Chandra Singh mention what had happened to Shafi?"

She nodded. "He said that the Pakistani had been shot dead while resisting arrest. Shafi managed to burn most of his papers, but there were enough left, together with the photostats, to prove beyond any doubt that he was spying for Pakistan."

"It fits the pattern," Mason reflected. "Even if Shafi had not chosen to resist arrest I doubt if Chandra Singh had any intentions of taking him alive. Neither would I have been taken alive if I had stayed in that room. And we know damned well how he hoped to find Panjit Sangh, dangling conveniently from the end of a rope The whole affair would have ended very neatly with no one left to ask any embarrassing questions or raise any awkward doubts. The Indians would be satisfied that they had recovered the photographs of their secret papers, and that they had cleaned up all the spies operating in Kashmir; and meanwhile Vandana will be escaping with the original photographs, together with all the additional material she must have had time to gather during the past few months. It was all worked out very nicely from the point of view of Vandana and Chandra Singh, and even now they are not doing so badly."

Shareena nodded and said in a dull

voice, "When Panjit was arrested the Captain of Military Police was there. We tried to convince him of the truth as you suggested, but he would not believe us. We pointed out the rope and the bruises on Panjit's neck where he had been attacked, but Chandra Singh was there and he said that the truth was that Panjit had tried to hang himself, and that I had stopped him from committing suicide and then made up the story. Everything we said Chandra Singh twisted round. The man is hateful. He is evil."

Mason smiled faintly and tried to comfort her. "We still have a chance," he said. "At least Panjit is alive, and I am free. Somehow I have to find out where Vandana has gone, follow her and bring her back." He paused thoughtfully, and then went on, "Let's try the process of elimination. There are only four ways of leaving Srinagar, one is by air, and there are three roads, south to Jammu, west to Pakistan, and north east to Ladakh. Am I right?"

Shareena nodded.

"Fine. Now we know that she must

have left during the night or early this morning. Could she have left by air?"

Shareena shook her head. "This time of year the tourist season is over. There are only a few flights a week in and out of Srinagar. There are no night flights, and I am sure that there would be no flight this morning I remember because I had to look up the timetables when I flew down to New Delhi to meet you."

Mason smiled. "That's progress. We can rule out the airport, so which is the most likely road? West into Pakistan seems least likely, she has no reason to go into that direction and she would certainly have difficulty in crossing the frontier."

Shareena nodded excitedly. "That is so. The frontier has been closed ever since the time of the war with Pakistan. Even to the south there is as yet only one crossing point that is open between our countries, that is at Ferozepore below Amritsar."

Mason smiled again. "Now we're getting warm. To escape from Srinagar she must have headed either north east into Ladakh, or south to Jammu. I doubt if she would face the Himalayas, so the odds are that she's gone south."

For the first time Shareena looked hesitant, he followed her gaze towards a wardrobe which he had inadvertently left half open during his earlier search.

"What's wrong?"

She smiled suddenly. "Paul, you are very clever, but you are still only a man. Did you not think to examine the clothes she left behind?"

Her meaning clicked like a switch in Mason's brain and he stood up and flung open the wardrobe. He had already looked through the things that Vandana had left behind, but only now did he see any meaning in the clothes themselves. They were all evening dresses, light summer saris, and lightweight slippers and shoes. Shareena came to his side and said, "Do you understand now? She has left behind all her summer clothes, the clothes she would need if she were going south. But there are no heavy winter clothes, she has taken those with her. She can only be going north."

Mason said softly. "So it's Ladakh, and then through one of the passes into China or Tibet." He looked down at the girl. "That's where I shall have to follow her. She won't be expecting any pursuit, and with luck I'll be able to catch up with her while she's still on the Indian side of the Himalayas. You can help me by finding me a car. I'll need transport of some kind and I can't move freely in Srinagar while the police are after my blood. If it's possible to hire one, I can give you the money."

Shareena said quietly, "My father owns a Land Rover. He is a road construction engineer and he needs the Land Rover to reach the sites where he is working. I know that he is not using the Land Rover today and so I shall bring it to you. If I were to ask his permission he would demand an explanation, and then I think he would refuse. So I shall simply take the Land Rover and leave my explanation in a written note. My father will be very angry with me when I return, but I know that he would not even dream of taking the matter to the police."

Mason said dubiously, "That's a generous offer, but when you have to face him your father might then decide to tell the police. He might feel that you have been very foolish and that it would be the best way of protecting you. Then the police would be chasing after me."

Shareena looked away from him and said even more quietly, "That will not happen, because I am coming with you. You will need the Land Rover, and also you will need me as an interpreter. You will find very few people who speak English north of Srinagar." She looked up then and finished, "There is nothing that I can do by staying here now that Panjit is under arrest, and the only way in which I can help him is by helping you. Please, Paul, do not argue."

Mason hesitated for a long moment. He could not guess at what dangers might lay ahead, and yet wherever the trail might lead he could be certain that it would be no place for a woman. At the same time he needed that Land Rover, and with no knowledge of the local language he had to have an interpreter to have any chance at all of following Vandana's movements. Shareena was waiting patiently, steadfastly for his reply, and finally he had to concede that she was right.

Shareena smiled her relief, and suddenly she put her arms around him, stretched up on her toes and kissed him quickly on the cheek. That was when he realized how deeply she was in love with Panjit Sangh.

14

The New Tibet

It was not safe for either of them to linger aboard the *Shalimar*, for not only were the two waiting *shikaras* likely to draw attention from the neighbouring houseboats, but also there was the distinct possibility that Chandra Singh would anticipate Mason's attempt to reach Vandana and send a party of police to investigate. Accordingly they returned to the shore and paid off their respective boatmen. They walked out of sight of the lake, and while Shareena hurried off to fetch the Land Rover Mason took refuge in a nearby restaurant. He knew that while the police were looking for him it would be too risky to accompany her, or even to stay on the streets, and the restaurant had the double advantage in that he could not only stay hidden, but could snatch a quick meal during her absence. After his hectic morning he was hungry, and being fully practised in taking his sleep and his meals when he could, he took full advantage of his opportunity to eat.

Three-quarters of an hour passed before Shareena returned. She entered the restaurant and took the seat beside him, and he noticed that she had changed from her attractive blue sari and now wore more business-like clothes, dark trousers and a heavy blue sweater, and laced-up leather boots. She noticed his reflective glance and said shyly, "Sometimes my father lets me accompany him. These are the clothes I wear on those occasions."

He smiled. "Very sensible. Did you get the Land Rover?"

"Yes, it is standing outside. Neither of my parents were at home, so that made it very easy for me. I left them a letter of explanation on the table, and also I borrowed some of my father's warmer clothes for you to wear. You are a little taller, but I think they will fit. You cannot go up into Ladakh wearing just a shirt and trousers. You would very quickly freeze."

Mason said wryly, "I'm getting ever deeper into your debt, and your father's. I can only hope that he's an understanding man."

Shareena said sadly, "He will be very angry. When I return perhaps he will beat me. But I know that he would never betray me, and that is all that is important."

Mason nodded, and after she had declined his invitation to eat he paid his bill and they went out to the Land Rover. He checked it over swiftly and noted that the tyres were hard, the oil and water levels were correct and the petrol gauge registered full. Shareena explained that she had already filled the tank. She shifted across the seat to make room for him behind the wheel and he climbed in beside her. The Land Rover was almost new and the engine purred sweetly as he started her up. He could not have been more fortunate in his choice of transport and he gave her a smile as they drove away.

He was wary as they drove out of Srinagar, but once they had left the city and the lake behind he began to relax. Ahead the narrow, tortuous road snaked through the valleys, climbing up into high, barren tableland, and then through the mighty barrier of the Himalayas on its two-hundred mile journey to Leh, the capital and only town of any size in Ladakh. Mason drove fast and said calmly, "Vandana probably left at dawn this morning, and that means that we're the best part of a day behind her."

Shareena nodded. "I think she would aim to get through the Zoji La, that is the mountain pass that is the entrance to Ladakh, and then she will probably spend the night at Kargil which is a town about half way along the route. Tomorrow she will drive on to Leh. That is if the road is clear and not blocked by snowdrifts. In mid-winter the Zoji La can be blocked by drifts up to eighty feet deep. We shall have to stop before the Zoji La. It would be dangerous to try and drive on through the night."

"Do you know this road well?"

"Fairly well," she answered. "My father worked on its construction. It was built to carry troops and supplies up into Ladakh when the Chinese first began to penetrate over our frontiers. I think that there are still two or three divisions of Indian troops stationed in Ladakh, facing the Chinese from our farthest outposts, and they depend upon this road for survival. It is a very vulnerable life-line, and last year the Pakistanis deliberately tried to cut it near Kargil during our more recent troubles. The road only goes as far as Leh, and then there are only tracks leading through the passes in the mountains."

Mason had to slow down to avoid a flock of sheep that were being driven across the road, and Shareena fell silent for a moment. The sheep were wild-looking and bleating noisily, and were chased by an even wilder-looking man wearing a sheepskin cloak and with two boys scrambling to assist him. They crossed the road but did not give the Land Rover a second glance. Mason drove on when they had passed. They had not yet left the green vale of Kashmir, but the road was climbing and they were getting ever nearer to the forbidding ramparts of the Himalayas. The great peaks frowned in icy splendour, and Mason said quietly, "Tell me something about Ladakh?"

Shareena looked towards the mountains for a moment, and then answered. "Ladakh is one of the most remote places left on the face of the earth. Beyond the Zoji La it is a terrible place. The mountains are a wilderness of ice and snow, and the valleys are bowls of whirling dust. It is very dry and arid and breathing becomes difficult. Only the hardest people can survive. Geographically Ladakh is part of Tibet, it is a northern continuation of the same high plateau of the Himalayas. It is sometimes called Little Tibet, and the people are mostly Khampas, and they are cousins of the Tibetans."

Mason said, "It must be one hell of a place to fight a war."

Shareena nodded soberly. "It is. During the winter of 1962 and 63, when the

232

worst of the border fighting occurred, everything was frozen up. Our soldiers fought with their hands frozen to the metal of their rifles. The grease in the mechanism of many of their weapons froze solid so that many guns could not be fired. The supply trucks were stopped with frozen batteries, and the meat and vegetables which our soldiers had to eat were frozen like chunks of iron. It was a terrible campaign, and the Chinese captured two thousand square miles of northern Ladakh before the cease-fire."

As she talked the peaks had closed around them. The road had crossed and now followed the course of a rushing, icy blue river that flowed down through the valley and the fearsome gorges. It was savagely beautiful, and ahead was the Zoji La, the barrier gateway to Ladakh. They had covered less than fifty miles, but the afternoon was merging into dusk and the western peaks were edged with a bright sunset glow of golden red. Mason was reluctant to stop, but he knew better than to try and cross the pass in darkness. He followed Shareena's advice and at the next cluster of houses that formed a village he stopped for the night. By then it was already dark.

* * *

They spent the night at a small tea house, and Mason was glad that he had Shareena with him to make the necessary negotiations. She was also able to report that a Land Rover carrying an Indian woman and two servants had passed through earlier in the day, and there was no longer any doubt that Vandana was ahead of them. They held a brief conference over a primitive evening meal of lentil soup, a vegetable curry and rice, and Mason decided that tomorrow he could probably carry on driving into the night in order to cut down even further on Vandana's lead. By the time they reached Leh they would only be a few hours behind, and in a town where strangers were rare it should not be too difficult to find her. Mason's only real worry was that Chandra Singh might suspect that his fellow-conspirator was being followed, and take the precaution of telephoning the army garrison at Leh to have them stopped. There was no reason why the Major should suspect that they had taken this road, but if he did they could so easily be halted and brought back. They had to hope that Chandra Singh was still concentrating his search for Mason in the bazaars of Srinagar.

★ ★ ★

After a night's sleep they arose when it was still dark, and the dawn was just a feeble grey light when they returned to the Land Rover. The air was sharp and cold and Mason had put on the warmer clothes that Shareena had borrowed for him, a thick sweater with a heavy coat and trousers, together with a fur cap with ear muffs that buttoned under his chin. Shareena had provided gloves for both of them.

The Land Rover was difficult to start, but once the engine fired she again ran smoothly. They left the cluster of tumbledown houses behind them and drove on up the gorge above the river. In the east the mountains were washed in the sun's blood, and ahead the road made its slow tortuous ascent to the Zoji La.

The pass lay at an altitude of eleven thousand five hundred feet, piercing the Himalayan range. Once through it they entered a different world, and the lush valleys of Kashmir were a past memory. Around them lay bleak landscapes of steep, frigid rocks, dry valleys filled with air-spun dust, and higher on the horizons desolate snow fields and great glacier slopes of gleaming ice. A cold wind blew, biting through their clothing and the air was sharp and frosty to their lungs. Mason had never before encountered a land that appeared so utterly hostile to human life, and he remembered that like neighbouring Tibet, Ladakh was situated on the roof of the world. There was nowhere higher than the Himalayan plateau.

It was a long tiring day of driving. During the morning the road forded several snow-fed streams, and Shareena mentioned quietly that after mid-day they would probably become impassable, flooded by melting snows from higher up the mountains. They passed no other traffic apart from a convoy of army supply trucks returning empty to Srinagar, and it was noon when they reached the small town of Kargil. They stopped to eat at a small rest house and again Shareena made some discreet enquiries. They learned that Vandana had stayed at this same rest house the previous night, and had continued on her journey to Leh shortly after dawn.

They continued after only a short stop, and Mason was a little relieved to get clear of Kargil without being challenged. Here they were very close to the disputed frontier with Pakistan, and he had half feared that a military checkpoint might turn him back. The road climbed up into another forbidding pass, even higher than the Zoji La, and then descended into the valley of the Indus river to follow the old caravan route to Leh. It took all the remaining hours of daylight to climb up and descend from the pass and the winds howled bitterly through the white wasteland. When they reached the Indus Mason was tired and weary, and despite his previous decision to drive on through the night his common sense ordered him to stop. Twelve hours of driving through this pitiless terrain was enough for any man, and he knew he had lopped several hours from Vandana's lead. By tomorrow he would catch up with her in Leh.

They stopped at the first small village in the Indus valley, and here Shareena was again able to get them an evening meal and accommodation at a small rest house. They retired early and Mason slept like the dead.

At dawn they drove on again, and after another three hours of following the river they arrived at the old trading post of Leh. Surrounded by a ring of bleak mountains the town was a step into the past. The ancient bazaar was dominated by a high, steep-walled palace which reminded Mason strongly of the old photographs of the Potala Palace in Lhasa, the one-time home of the Dalai Lama of Tibet before the Red Chinese had crushed that country beneath their marching armies. The faces in the narrow main street were also reminiscent of Tibet, broad Mongoloid faces with narrow eyes, the chins of the men adorned by scraggy wisps of beard. Donkeys and mules provided the main transport, and Mason saw one shaggy, long-haired animal which he suddenly realized was a yak. The place was primitive, but there were a few scattered trucks and jeeps to mark the presence of the army garrison, and Shareena told him that Leh possessed the highest air-strip in India.

They left the Land Rover in the main street, and together they went in search of Vandana. Mason would have preferred to leave Shareena behind just in case he was unexpectedly faced by Zakir and Kalam, but again he was almost wholly dependant upon her knowledge of the language. They enquired at three small guest houses, none of them really large enough to be dignified by the title of hotels, and learned that Vandana had stayed the night at the third. However, she had again left shortly after dawn. The owner of the guest house was dubious about answering questions, but tempted by money he answered them nonetheless. He showed Mason the Land Rover which Vandana had left behind in his yard, and explained that she was now on foot. Her servants had bought extra clothing and supplies, and had hired a Ladakhi guide to take them even farther north.

When Shareena translated Mason rasped his fingers slowly across his unshaven jaw, and then asked, "Is it possible that she'll try to cross the Himalayas into China at this time of year? Will the passes be open?"

Shareena looked doubtful, but she nodded. "It is late, but not too late, and if she has continued north she can have no other objective. She will either turn east towards Chinese Tibet, or she will head for the Karakoram pass into China itself. These are the old trade routes."

"Then I'll have to follow," Mason said grimly. "Where can I hire a guide?"

Shareena spoke with the hotel-owner for a moment and then turned back.

"He says we should ask in the bazaar. There is a man called Tsaro, who is the

240

brother of the guide hired by Vandana. If we can find him he will know where his brother has gone, and perhaps he will guide us." She saw the protest he was about to make and finished sharply. "Us, Paul! You will still need me to translate for you."

Mason hesitated. She was young and she was vulnerable, she might delay him, and then prove the weak chink in his armour when he met up with his enemies. But she was also in love and would do everything she could to help him bring about the release of Panjit Sangh. Already she had proved invaluable, and without her he would still be stranded in Srinagar instead of just a few hours behind his quarry. He finally nodded and said, "All right, let's go and find the bazaar."

15

The High Passes

Tsaro proved to be one of the wildest-looking ruffians that Mason had ever seen. His broad, Mongoloid face was a wrinkled yellowish brown, and his hair hung down his back in a long, black and greasy pigtail. He wore an embroidered fur cap and an ankle length woollen coat gathered at the waist by a rope of hair. He was small, sturdy, aged about forty, and he smelled. After an hour of searching and asking endless questions in the narrow dirt streets of the bazaars they found him sipping a glass of black tea in a small eating house.

Again it was Shareena who did all the talking, while Mason could only wait and listen. Once Tsaro had reluctantly admitted his identity they sat opposite him across a rough wooden table, and Mason saw blank hostility on his face as Shareena explained what they wanted. The Indian girl talked earnestly, but despair began to creep into her tone and at last she turned back to Mason.

"Paul, he says that he does not know anything about his brother. I do not think he will help us at all."

Mason said quietly, "I expected that. It's a certain bet that his brother is leading Vandana into the mountains without the knowledge of the police and military authorities here in Leh. If the authorities were informed Vandana would be stopped and brought back, and his brother would be in serious trouble. You'll have to convince Tsaro that by helping us he won't be betraying his brother. Convince him that we are friends of Vandana and that our intentions are simply to join up with her party so that we can all continue into China together."

Shareena nodded and then tried again. At first the stubborn Ladakhi would only grunt and shake his head, but eventually he began to argue with her, asking sharp guttural questions, Shareena turned abruptly to Mason and said,

"Paul, you will have to show him some money."

Mason smiled, and now that the barrier of family loyalty had been overcome he knew that they had bought a guide.

He brought out his wallet and opened it to show the notes inside. They were badly crinkled after their wetting in the Jhelum but they were still serviceable and Mason had come well supplied. Previous experience had told that hard cash was always necessary on any mission of this kind, and the only drawback was that this time it was coming from his own pocket instead of through the pay office of Naval Intelligence. Tsaro examined the notes dubiously and then nodded.

There followed another thirty minutes of emphatic discussion, but now it was Tsaro who did most of the talking. He spoke to Shareena but mostly his dark, slit eyes would keep flickering towards Mason's face. Finally Shareena turned to translate.

"He says that his brother is taking Vandana towards the Karakoram pass. They are carrying heavy packs of supplies and we shall have to do the same." She hesitated, and then added, "The amount of supplies she is carrying will not be enough for her to travel right through the mountains, so Vandana must be aiming for one of the advance Chinese outposts, somewhere where she can pick up more supplies and possibly a troop escort into China."

Mason drummed his fingers thoughtfully on the scratched surface of the table. "We shall have to catch her before that happens. What time did she leave?"

Shareena translated the question, and then the answer.

"They left at about nine o'clock this morning. Tsaro says that we can leave at dawn tomorrow."

Mason shook his head. "There are still several hours of daylight left, and we can't afford to waste any time. Tell him we must leave in an hour. Offer more money if you have to."

Shareena nodded and spoke again to Tsaro. The Ladakhi protested violently and another argument ensued. It lasted ten minutes and then Tsaro shrugged eloquently, slapped his hands upon the table and glared at Mason.

Shareena said, "He will be ready in two hours. He has to buy supplies and he needs time to go home and tell his wife that he is going on the trip. He wants forty rupees per day for his services, including a full day's pay for today. And he says that he will need two hundred rupees in advance to pay for the supplies. I think he is charging highly, but he knows our need is urgent."

Mason nodded resignedly, and began to count out the money for the supplies.

★ ★ ★

Two and a half hours later they left Leh, moving on foot along a narrow track that avoided the main route north. Tsaro had led them by a devious back route out of the town to avoid any interest in their departure, and for the first hour or so he kept up a fast, hurrying pace over the rough, stony ground. They climbed quickly into the bleak brown mountains, passing many scattered caves that had once been inhabited by monks, but seeing few signs of life. Behind them Leh was an unimpressive huddle of dull houses, with only the high walls of the old palace and the single dome of a small mosque outstanding. They saw a distant glimpse of the airstrip and then their path led through a pass into the mountains and the plain was hidden behind them. Piles of white stones had marked their route, small cairns set up by Buddhist pilgrims who had passed before them, both to mark the way and to thank God for a safe passage.

Both Mason and Tsaro were carrying heavy, square sixty-pound packs, supported by leather straps across their shoulders. Shareena carried a smaller rucksack which she had taken from their Land Rover before they had left the vehicle beside Vandana's in the guest house yard. Cold, blustery winds had slammed into them as they climbed away from Leh, and it was a relief to leave the open country behind. Shareena was panting slightly and Mason helped her whenever the going became rough. Tsaro looked back at them from time to time, but his face was expressionless and he maintained the same gruelling pace. They had impressed upon him that they wished to catch up with the party being guided by his brother, but Mason guessed that the Ladakhi's main concern was to get well clear of Leh and any possibility of being stopped and questioned.

Once they entered the pass they were surrounded by fierce barriers of brown and grey rock, and the way became steeper and more rugged. The air was thin which made breathing difficult, and as it was now getting late in the day the air was much colder. They rounded a corner and a wind howled abruptly into their faces, blowing directly down the pass. Shareena fumbled to pull down the ear muffs of the fur cap she was now wearing and buttoned the straps under her chin. Mason followed her example and was glad that she had been able to provide him with the necessary clothing. All that he had needed to buy before setting out were a pair of strong boots to replace his soft-soled shoes, and the presence of the army in the area had made them easily obtainable in the bazaar.

For another two hours they struggled on and Shareena began to stumble more frequently. Mason knew she needed to rest but Tsaro was still forcing the pace and he was reluctant to call the guide to a halt. Nightfall was coming fast and they had to find some place of refuge before darkness. The shadows tightened around them and then the stars came out, giving a ghostly gleam to the distant snowfields and the white peaks. The wind still drove into their teeth, adding to the difficulty of breathing in the rarified air, and Mason too began to feel the strain.

At last a stone hut appeared, standing just off the track, and here Tsaro indicated that they would spend the night. They lowered their packs and Shareena even managed a faint smile as Mason helped her. She shivered in the bitter wind and Mason calculated that they must be at an altitude of at least thirteen thousand feet. The night sky was as beautiful as he had ever seen it, but the land around them was savage and freezing.

Tsaro entered the hut and lit some candles from their packs to give them a small amount of light. The interior of the hut was bare and blackened, and the floor was hard-packed dirt. In one corner of the flat roof was a chimney hole, and beneath it the Ladakhi busied himself in lighting a small fire, using chips of dried animal dung that he had gathered along the last mile. Mason lifted their packs inside, but there was little else that he could do to help so he sat with Shareena beside the fire. While they warmed themselves and tried to thaw out Tsaro prepared them a makeshift meal. They ate the hot, greasy stew that he finally offered them without daring to ask what was in it, and washed it down with scalding hot tea. Afterwards Tsaro built up their fire with what little fuel was left, and they huddled around it and tried to sleep. They had a blanket each to wrap around themselves and slept fully clothed.

* * *

Despite the fact that they were both weary they woke early. The fire had burned out, the temperature was deep below zero and the gnawing cold had again eaten into their bones. The winds were shrieking noisily around their lonely mountain hut, and as a final discomfort the air was filled with the strong, unwashed smell of their guide. They lay awake until dawn made a grey disc of the chimney hole in the roof, and then Tsaro grunted and began to stir. After a moment he got up, scratched himself thoroughly and then went outside. When he returned he made more of the hot black tea, and after a breakfast of biscuits they retied their packs and moved on. The sky was grey and clear but the sun had not yet appeared above the eastern ice peaks.

It proved another gruelling day. The track that they followed soon merged with the main trade route towards the distant Karakoram pass, but although the trail was a little wider and easier there was no relief from the biting winds. They were still climbing higher and even when the sun rose the temperature stayed below zero. They had to keep breathing fast to extract enough oxygen from the thin air, and every muscle ached beneath the weight of their packs. Shareena did not complain, but Mason knew that she was struggling hard to keep up and he was worried that she would burn up all her strength. Tsaro trudged steadily in the lead, slightly bowed beneath his pack, but showing no sign of any discomfort.

Around them was a scrambled wilderness of white snow-fields, pierced by bleak out-thrusts of bare rock, and in the distance lofty peaks were cloaked in glaciers of ice. The winds swirled up storms of fine snow, and howled like laughing demons among the crags. Underneath their feet the track was treacherous and slippery, covered with loose stones and patches of frozen slush and ice. Once mule trains had used it to trade with China, and in places Mason wondered how even a mule could have kept its footing.

They made one stop in mid morning, and another longer one at noon when Tsaro again provided a meal. This time he could find no fuel for a fire, and so they ate cold meat from tins. Shareena sat down thankfully for the rest, and Mason guessed from the strained lines of her face that she was suffering from a headache. There was a dull throbbing in his own temples, caused most probably by the high altitude and he had a deep feeling of sympathy. He wished that he had left her in Leh, but knew that even now she would not turn back, even if it had been possible.

The cold soon forced them into movement again and they pushed on, but it was only a few minutes later that they rounded a buttress of rock and found another of the small stone huts. This was the third since the hut where they had spent the night, the previous two had showed no signs of recent use, but in this one there were ashes from a fire only hours old. Tsaro pointed them out with a confident finger and Shareena translated his words.

"He says that this hut was used last night. Four people used it, which means that it must have been Vandana and her party."

Mason smiled wearily. "Then we're catching up. We're now only half a day behind. Possibly less if she made a late start this morning." He paused, and then added, "Now that we've got some shelter I think we can afford to rest for a bit."

Shareena faltered, and then shook her head.

"No, Paul. We are still a long way behind, and you must not think of me. I shall be all right."

Mason studied her doubtfully, and then nodded. He knew that even though her strength was failing her courage would carry her a long way yet. Either courage or love, or perhaps the two were one. He didn't really know. He looked to Tsaro and indicated that they were ready to move on.

They left the hut and toiled on through the afternoon, fighting the cold, and the winds, and their own weariness. The effects of the increasing altitude told more heavily on their bodies, weighing down their sluggish limbs, and the lack of oxygen dulling minds as well as muscle. They fought their way through

254

the heights of another freezing pass where piled snowdrifts caused them to sink above their knees, and where at one point they were floundering up to their waists. Mason helped the girl as much as possible, and finally he split up the contents of her pack between himself and the guide. Tsaro made no comment and seemed unconcerned by the extra weight.

There was still over an hour of daylight left when they came upon another of the crude stone huts, and here Tsaro unslung his pack. Shareena began weakly to protest, but the guide merely shrugged as he answered and then turned away. Shareena looked at Mason and had to breathe deeply before she could speak again.

"He says that there isn't another hut that we can reach before nightfall. We must stop here."

Mason put his arm around her shoulders and smiled as he tried to console her.

"Don't worry about it. Vandana must be moving a lot slower than we are, and we'll catch up to her in a couple of days.

She has no need to drive herself hard."

Shareena hesitated a moment, and then nodded reluctantly. Her face was troubled and Mason knew that she was still worrying about Panjit Sangh, for if Vandana succeeded in escaping into China there was no hope for the young Lieutenant. And there was no definite way in which he could comfort her, for despite his outward optimism there was no guarantee that they could close up with their quarry before Vandana contacted one of the forward Chinese border posts. A patrol might even have been sent to meet her, for there was no way of knowing how deeply the Chinese had penetrated into Ladakh.

* * *

That night followed the pattern of the one before, except that they were higher, the temperature was lower, and the winds howled even more wildly through the freezing darkness. However, weariness helped them to sleep, and when they awoke just before dawn they were stiff in every limb and muscle.

They faced their second day on another breakfast of tea and biscuits, for Tsaro had been wholly unimaginative in buying their supplies, and again continued their trek across the Himalayan plateau. They were now heading away from the Himalayas towards the equally forbidding ranges of the Karakoram, behind which lay China. The altitude and the bitter winds were again their constant enemies, and they were encountering more patches of frozen slush and ice, and delaying drifts of hard-crusted snow. Mason started the day by limping badly, for his new boots had blistered his heels, but after an hour his feet were so numb with cold that he could walk without pain. They had dumped Shareena's rucksack after its contents had been shared into the remaining two packs, so now the going was just a little bit easier for the girl.

After three hours they came to another of the rough stone huts that were spaced out for the use of travellers along the way, and here their spirits were given a new boost. There were recent ashes in the fireplace and there was no doubt that Vandana and her companions had stayed here during the night. Mason calculated that they could now be only three hours behind, and Shareena managed to smile.

They rested briefly, ate some more biscuits and tinned meat, and then pushed on into the gale force winds. They made good progress for an hour, for the knowledge that they were gaining on their quarry had restored Shareena's failing strength. Then she began to flag again and their pace slowed. She struggled gamely at Mason's side, relying heavily on his arm, and when they halted again at noon she almost collapsed on the icy ground.

They found a small hollow where there was some relief from the winds, and while Tsaro brewed up hot tea, using some fuel he had found in the last hut for a fire, Mason did his best to bring Shareena back to life. He removed her boots and gloves and massaged warmth back into her hands and feet to save them from frost-bite, stopping only when the returning blood made her wince with the tingling pain. Afterwards he performed the same treatment for himself, even though he knew that life for his numbed feet meant more agony from the raw patches left by his blisters.

The last hours of the day were another freezing ordeal that made their bodies ache and their minds reel. The winds battered more strongly into their faces until Tsaro fell back so that he and Mason could help Shareena between them. They struggled on, half carrying the girl, until at last the guide pointed out the hut where they were to spend the night. Mason was feeling slightly sick and his brain was slow, but the instinct for caution was still there and he knew that it was just possible that the hut was already inhabited. Vandana might have chosen to halt early for the night, and he had no desire to stumble unwittingly into her two servants. He gestured to Tsaro to remain behind with Shareena and went forward alone.

As soon as the Ladakhi was behind him and unable to see what he was doing he fumbled inside his heavy coat and drew out Panjit Sangh's army revolver. His hands were cold inside his fur gloves and he almost dropped it, and he needed both hands to hold it level in front of him. He approached the hut slowly but there were no signs of life, and when he kicked open the door he found it empty. He was not sure whether to be relieved or disappointed.

He pushed the revolver back inside his coat out of sight and unslung his pack. When he turned round Tsaro had come up to join him, still supporting Shareena, and there was a puzzled half suspicious look on the wrinkled, yellowish face. Mason smiled to reassure him that everything was all right, and hoped that he was not capable of thinking too deeply. They were wholly dependant upon Tsaro, and if the Ladakhi had any doubts that they were not friends of his brother's party then he could so easily lead them in useless circles until their supplies ran low and they had to return.

★ ★ ★

They spent a cold, comfortless night, and began their third day once more at dawn. They were refreshed, but Mason knew that Shareena would only last a few hours before she began to falter. During the past few days she had drained her strength and now she was definitely slowing their progress. They had started by steadily overhauling Vandana, but now he calculated that they must be barely keeping pace behind her, and it was even possible that they were losing ground.

He was faced with a grim choice. Either to stay with Shareena, and continue to hope that they would eventually overtake their quarry; or to leave her behind with the guide and the supplies, and hope that he could swiftly catch up with Vandana unladen and alone. The latter course seemed to offer the best chance of success, and he would not have to worry about which side Tsaro would support when the pursuit ended, but he also had to face the fact that without Tsaro he could easily stray off the right trail and lose himself in the

261

wind-driven wilderness, where without supplies he would perish and freeze.

Normally he was capable of weighing the facts of any given situation and making a fast decision, but again the altitude and the lack of oxygen was dulling his brain and he found it difficult to think. Then abruptly Tsaro halted in front of him and he almost blundered into the guide's back. He had to shake his head to clear it and then squint his eyes against the icy wind. Tsaro had half turned towards him and was staring down intently at the stony, frozen ground. He moved away to their left and then came back. His coat was flapping in the wind and he reached one hand inside it to scratch, still staring down at the trail.

"What's wrong?" Mason demanded.

Shareena translated and Tsaro answered in a dubious voice, still looking down at his feet. Shareena said slowly.

"Paul, he says that Vandana and her party have turned off the main trail. They've branched off to the left."

Mason blocked the wind from his eyes

with his hand and tried to read the signs. There were faint indications of what might have been a path to their left, but he could see no tracks to show that it had been recently used. He looked uncertainly at the guide.

"Is he sure?"

Shareena asked again, and this time Tsaro looked up and nodded. Mason could not detect any duplicity in the yellow-brown face, and so he said decidedly, "All right. Where they go — we go. We'll turn to the left."

Shareena spoke again to Tsaro and a short discussion ensued. Then she looked up at Mason.

"Paul, he says that there is nothing to the left. Nothing at all. Just a minor pass that leads to nowhere. This is the main trail to the Karakoram pass. He cannot understand why they have turned away."

Mason said grimly, "It doesn't matter. If he's sure that Vandana took this route, then we have to follow."

Shareena nodded, and repeated his decision to Tsaro. The guide still looked

263

uncertain, but after a moment he turned to the left and began to follow the new track. They left the main trail behind and plunged even farther north into the unmapped desolation of Ladakh.

16

The Poised Threat

Their new route was barely a track at all and Mason and Shareena could only follow blindly where Tsaro led. Mason looked for any signs that might have been left by Vandana's party but there was nothing, the wind-swirled snow had blotted everything out. The winds turned any efforts at communication into a disjointed yelling match, and in any case Shareena was too breathless to translate, so Mason could ask no questions. He could only trust to Tsaro's unerring instinct. He did not doubt that the Ladakhi could read signs which he could not see, perhaps a scratch on the ice or a stone dislodged from its frozen seat in the iron hard earth, and his only worry was that Tsaro might be deliberately leading them astray. Either way they could not hope to catch up to Vandana without him, and so they had no choice but to trust the guide.

They were climbing again, and heading for a gap between two ice-coated mountains. A fearsome maze of jagged black rocks barred their path, rearing high out of the snow in a bleak, lunar landscape. Tsaro picked a weaving path through the maze and all around them the wind whistled and moaned through the hollowed crags. It was a lifeless world, and Mason found it difficult to realize that somewhere in this remote and pitiless region several divisions of Indian and Chinese troops were crouched in icy dug-outs, and alert for any renewal of the border war. Their existence must be little short of hell, and the land for which they prepared to fight was worthless.

Mason's mind struggled back to the decision he had been trying to make before they left the main trail, but slowly he realized that it had been taken out of his hands. Here he could barely distinguish a track at all and it would be suicide to try and move ahead of the guide. It was out of the question to even consider leaving Shareena behind, and so all three of them had to continue together.

The frozen earth gave way to knee deep snow which slowed their progress even more, taxing their strength as they floundered in Tsaro's wake. Mason could still see no tracks of a previous passage, and again his suspicions that Tsaro might be leading them in circles came rushing back. Then he glanced behind and saw that the wind was filling up their own tracks as it gusted across the snow, and he felt reassured once more. The last suspicion died when Tsaro halted in the shelter of a massive rock and pointed out the spot where Vandana and her companions had rested for a while.

They stopped to regain their breath, and again Mason attended to the task of massaging warmth back into Shareena's hands and feet, and then his own feet to protect them from frostbite. Tsaro watched, but seemed as fit and vigorous as when they had started out. The cold did not seem to bother him, although Mason and Shareena found that the winds knifed easily through their heavy woollen sweaters and coats. In this arctic world they badly needed furs.

After only a short rest Shareena insisted that she was capable of going on, and so they renewed their trek towards the dip of the distant pass. The sky above them was a watery blue, but if there was any heat from the sun it was swept away by the constant winds. The temperature remained deep below zero. Whenever it was possible to see any distance ahead Mason bridged his eyes with his gloved hands and searched for any signs of movement across the snow and ice, but there was nothing there. It was a lonely, empty landscape, a mountainous playground for the tempestuous air currents that blustered and moaned.

They had to stop again at noon to rest and eat, and Tsaro boiled up water for more of the scalding tea that was their only luxury and relief. He had found a pile of frozen mule droppings shortly before leaving the main trail, and was able to use them for fuel to build a small fire. Wood was nonexistent. A jumble of rocks gave them shelter, but after half an hour they retied their packs and emerged into the winds to return to their gruelling battle against the hostile elements.

For another hour they moved stubbornly forward. The frozen mountains loomed closer on either side and they ascended steadily towards the pass. Several times they floundered into deep snow drifts that buried them to the neck or chest, but for the most part Tsaro managed to pick a path where the snow was only knee or thigh deep. Mason continued to search ahead, squinting through narrowed, aching eyes, but there was nothing to break the monotony of rocks and ice. Then abruptly, late in the afternoon, Tsaro stopped and pointed.

Mason had to bridge his eyes again, feeling the tears trickle and freeze against his face as they were stung by the bitter wind. He stared for several moments, and then he picked them out, four tiny black figures moving slowly into the mouth of the pass. They were about a quarter of a mile distant, and he saw them only briefly before a squall of lifted snow blotted them out.

He had the normal altitude headache, but this time he reached a decision without hesitation. Now that he could see his quarry he no longer needed the guide, and he turned to Shareena with a weary, unshaven smile.

"It has to be Vandana. There are four figures. Herself, Zakir and Kalam, and the guide. I'm going after them alone, while you find somewhere to rest or else come up slowly with Tsaro. Tell him that I don't want to leave you alone, and that once I catch up with the other party I'll tell them to wait. That should satisfy any questions."

Shareena nodded, but her face showed pale signs of alarm. They had to shout to talk and her voice was hoarse as she answered, "I understand, Paul. But what will you do alone. They are four to one."

Mason said grimly, "Zakir and Kalam have got to die. I can't bring them back as well. We know that they are both murderers so my conscience won't trouble me on that score. What happens to their guide all depends on his own actions, but I don't expect him to be any trouble. Vandana I intend to bring back." He smiled and added. "Remember, I'm carrying the Lieutenant's revolver."

He unslung his pack as he spoke, and reluctantly Shareena explained to Tsaro. The guide answered briefly and a new look of worry showed in her eyes.

"Paul, he says he will catch up with the other party. And then he and his brother can come back for us."

Mason hesitated, and then said flatly, "Tell him I prefer him to look after you, and don't let him argue."

Shareena obeyed, but Tsaro made no more protest. He merely shrugged and began to move their packs into a sheltered hollow. Mason rested his gloved hand for a moment on Shareena's shoulder, and reassured her with another smile.

"Don't worry," he said. "I'll be back."

She nodded dumbly and then he turned away. She watched him plunge forward into the teeth of the wind, his shoulders hunched forward and his coat flapping wildly. Her head was aching and there was sick worry in her heart, but after a moment her utter weariness forced her to turn away and join Tsaro, almost falling beside the guide and their packs. She was afraid for Mason, and she was so desperately afraid for Panjit Sangh. So much so that there was no fear left to cause any reflections upon her own fate if Mason should fail to return.

Mason could no longer distinguish the four members of Vandana's party against the ice and snow, but he was close enough to the pass entrance to be able to aim directly for it, and had no major fears of losing his way. Without the crushing pack on his back he had a new freedom of movement that enabled him to move fast, and now that the end was in sight he had fresh heart for the last part of the pursuit. His enemies had been moving at a tired, crawling pace, and he guessed that like Shareena, Vandana must be weakening and slowing her party down. Mason knew that he must be overhauling them rapidly.

After half an hour he was nearing

the mouth of the pass and still he had not caught a second glimpse of his quarry. He guessed that they must have entered into the pass itself and tried to increase his pace. A blunder that cost him ten minutes in trying to escape from a deep snowdrift. The walls of the pass towered over him, and the climb became very steep. Icy rocks littered the path and several times he slipped. He was tiring after his initial spurt, but then he rounded a great buttress of black rock that almost blocked the pass and again his hopes surged. The four members of the fugitive party were clearly visible only a few hundred yards ahead.

Mason drew back into a sheltered cleft and clumsily drew the heavy revolver from inside his coat. He checked that the chamber spun freely but his body heat had prevented the weapon from freezing up. He fitted it carefully into his gloved right hand, flicked off the safety, and then moved forward once more.

There was no need to make any attempts at silence, for the sound of the winds blotted out any noise that he might have made. His presence would only be noticed when one of the four figures ahead glanced round, and he hurried to close the gap as much as possible before that happened.

The four figures ahead were now at the far end of the pass, which was acting like a wind tunnel for a screaming, high velocity gale. Three of them were bowed down beneath heavy packs, and the struggle to make headway required all their energy. The fourth member of the party was unladen, but trailing several paces in the rear. All of them were shapeless in thick winter clothing, but Mason knew that the unladen member of the party must be Vandana.

He closed the gap to within two hundred yards. By then the lead party had left the far mouth of the pass and were veering left to encircle a great, glass-like ridge of ice that lay like a barrier wall across their path. Mason was half way through the pass, moving as fast as he dared across treacherous icy rocks that could easily spell a fall and a broken leg. He was overhauling fast, and then the last of the four slow figures glanced round.

He saw her stop and immediately slowed his pace. He doubted whether she could recognize him yet, and there was a chance that he could get close enough to act before she sensed any danger. He saw the remaining three figures stop and turn round, but continued to advance at a steady walking pace. He had dropped the revolver to his side where it was less noticeable, and in an effort to confuse them he casually raised his left hand and waved. Then the unexpected happened. He had assumed the lead man to be the guide, and had supposed him to be holding a short staff to help negotiate the rough ground. But he was mistaken, the staff was raised and a sharp crack echoed above the howl of the winds.

Mason instinctively jerked to one side, skidding and sprawling clumsily on the ice. He realized then that the last act of the drama was not going to be as simple as he had first supposed, for either Zakir or Kalam was carrying a rifle. His heart was thumping as he scrambled behind a shield of rocks, but although he had retained his grip on the revolver he did not attempt to return the fire. He knew the range was too short. The rifle cracked again and the bullet ricocheted off the wall of the pass, six feet to his left and high above. It was the second wide miss and he guessed that the man holding the rifle was handicapped by cold and numbed hands. That did not necessarily give him any edge, for his own hands were stiff and slow.

His sluggish brain tried to balance the implications of those two shots, and he cursed the throbbing headache caused by the altitude. He was sure that Vandana could not have recognized him from the distance, which meant that she was prepared to shoot at any stray traveller who might follow her path. Would she now continue, hoping that he had been driven back, or would she send Zakir and Kalam to ensure that he was dead? If she chose the latter course then the odds were on his side, for he could let the two servants get within revolver range and shoot them down. They would not expect him to be armed.

He edged cautiously to one side of the concealing rocks and risked a swift glance forward. The wind struck into his eyes and he found that he was gritting his teeth. Nobody was coming back to see what had happened to him, and instead Vandana and her companions were moving away. He hesitated, realizing that if he followed now she would have no doubt that he was an enemy. Yet at the same time he had no choice but to follow. The afternoon was getting late and he had to finish the job and rejoin Shareena and Tsaro before nightfall. If he failed he would be separated from both parties and would perish during the freezing night. He stood up grimly and renewed the pursuit.

After a moment Vandana looked round and stopped her small party for the second time. The rifle cracked, but although Mason made a pretence of dodging to one side he did not attempt to scramble into hiding. He was confident that none of them could handle the rifle with any accuracy until their hands had

277

thawed, and his main hope now was to tempt them into wasting ammunition. Another bullet skewered splinters of ice off the wall of the pass, but then Vandana stopped the rifleman from any further shooting. She had obviously seen that the bullets were being wasted, and after a short conference she and her companions resumed their march. Mason kept pace behind, hoping to draw more shots but not daring to get too close to the rifle. From this distance his revolver was useless, and while he could not close the gap the position was stalemate.

He wondered why Vandana did not send Kalam back to deal with him, for he was almost sure that it was Kalam who was using the rifle. The short, stocky figure who was now leading had to be Tsaro's brother, and there was something about the third man's stance and movements that identified him as Zakir. The question puzzled Mason for a moment and then his dulled brain provided the answer. Vandana appreciated the same fact that had occurred to him only a moment ago;

namely that the approaching darkness and the elements would deal with him in a very short time and that there was no need to delay her progress. As the situation now stood he was no threat.

His instinct was to force the issue, to push ahead until he was within revolver range and hope that he was capable of firing a straighter shot than Kalam. The urge to push the ordeal to almost any conclusion was strong, but then sanity fought its way back into his pain drugged mind and he knew that in no circumstances would a revolver ever be a match for a rifle. There had to be another way.

He searched the terrain ahead, and slowly saw a possible answer. The pass had opened out and the trail lay left to avoid the barrier ridge of ice, but as far as he could see the sheer wall of the pass turned right again behind the ridge, forcing a circling loop in the trail. Vandana and her three porters were moving at a snail's pace because of their packs, and there was a chance that if he could scale the ridge he could cut them off on the far side.

Dubiously he studied the face of the ice-coated ridge. It looked smooth and impassable, but in places there were clefts and ledges. His commando training had taught him how to climb, but on slippery ice and in these winds there was a definite danger of a fatal fall. He hesitated, and then veered off the narrow trail, climbing up through scattered rocks to the base of the ridge where he could make a closer inspection.

The ridge presented over sixty feet of hazardous climbing, and if there had been any other way he would not have attempted it. But there was no other way. He was now out of sight of his quarry and the chances were that his movements would be unseen. If he reached the far side he could lay in ambush and he did not doubt his ability to shoot down both Zakir and Kalam before they could make any attempt to defend their mistress. Only the ridge itself barred his way.

He reached his decision and thrust his revolver back inside his coat. He drew off one glove and fumbled inside his trouser pocket for his clasp knife and used his teeth to open the blade. He drew on the glove once more and with the knife in his hand he started on his climb. He had already picked his path and where the ice was too smooth he painstakingly stabbed shallow holds with the point of his knife. Once he made the mistake of returning it to his teeth while he used both hands to pull himself up past a difficult shoulder of rock, and the steel blade froze to his lips. He wrenched it free, and a small patch of skin came away with the blade. His lower lip smarted badly but was soon numbed by the cold.

He inched his way slowly upwards, not daring to hurry on the treacherous ice. If the climb had been sheer it would have been impossible with only the clasp knife to aid him, but mercifully the rock-face beneath the ice was angled inwards. Below him black rocks broke through the hard-crusted snow and the winds beat at his face and whipped through his clothing. Without the warming exertion of fast movement the cold began tightening around his limbs and muscles and he could no longer feel his feet. He had to continually glance down to make sure that he was placing them in the right position, and he was thankful that he now had the nailed boots in place of his former soft shoes.

Half way up the face of the ridge he encountered a blank stretch between a ledge and a higher cleft with no holds whatsoever. He was faced with ten feet of glassy ice and it took him over fifteen minutes to chip out the necessary holds and drag himself upwards. He knew that he was losing time but still he dared not hurry. His hands were now so frozen that he had to crouch in the low cleft and beat them violently together to restore some small measure of warmth. When at last he looked up he saw that the cleft continued to the crest of the ridge some fifteen feet above, and he used it to provide his path to the top. He was still using the clasp knife to chip at the ice and his arm was beginning to ache, and when he was still five feet from the top his dulled fingers lost their grip and the knife fell from his gloved hand. It clattered past him on the icy rock, and then it was lost.

Mason cursed but he was long past the point of no return, and after a moment he dragged himself a little higher. His handholds ran out and he groped helplessly for a grip, first with his right hand and then his left. There was nothing and he had to shift his position around the cleft and try again. His gloved fingers touched a knob of rock and he gambled on finding another hold for his free hand as he drew himself up. The hold was there and a moment later he was able to haul himself out of the cleft and on to the top of the ridge.

A howling wind blasted into his face as he emerged, blinding him and all but kicking him back into space and the long fall into the pass. It rushed at him like the freezing slipstream of an express train and he crawled into it with his head bowed to take the full force on his shoulders. He sprawled flat for a moment with his face buried in crusted snow, and it seemed impossible that he could ever rise again. He made the effort and the wind screamed around him in demented fury. He could not see but he sensed that there was a wide valley before him which allowed the winds to build up into almost hurricane force as they swept to the mountains. He had to protect his face and peer beneath his sheltering arm as he stumbled down the slope of the ridge to where a deeply-seated boulder offered him a merciful wind-break.

When he had recovered his breath and his spinning senses he was able to distinguish the trail below. This slope of the ridge was not so fearsome and he judged that he could succeed in getting down. He searched for his enemies, praying that he was in time, and then saw the four bowed figures just struggling into sight on the far left. They were emerging from the gap between the far hump of the ridge and the sheer wall of the pass. He was not as far ahead as he had hoped, but providing they did not look up to see him make his descent he was confident that he could get down to the trail in time to lay in wait.

He started to climb down, moving slowly because of the unsure footing and harassed by the fiendish winds. The sky was darkening, but it was not the starlit darkness of nightfall, and he realized abruptly that the weather was deteriorating into a storm. The knowledge made him hesitate and look north, again protecting his slitted eyes from the freezing winds.

That was when he became still. He could distinguish the broad valley that lay before him, and despite the tears being forced from his tortured eyes he suddenly realized that the valley was occupied. There were long rows of circular tents pitched far below him, and hordes of tiny little ant-like figures scurrying between the lines. He saw that they could only be troops and calculated that there must be at least two divisions. For a moment his astonished mind refused to accept what he saw, and he wondered if the effects of the altitude were playing tricks on his oxygen-starved brain.

And then he saw the machines. They were neither trucks nor gun-carriers nor tanks, but strange, grotesque vehicles that appeared to combine the operations of all three. Two of them were manoeuvring almost directly below him and he watched as they lurched methodically across the valley floor. Each machine travelled on three great ball-like wheels, each one separately articulated so that they wriggled around obstacles in almost obscene strides. The wheels were a mass of steel spikes, reminiscent of deep-sea mines, and at first he could not see their purpose. Then he realized that each spike was angled so that on striking level ground it would be harmlessly pushed back into its slot in the ball wheel, but on encountering any obstruction on its downward revolution it would catch hold and drag the wheel up and over whatever barred the way. One of the two machines was loaded with a large field gun, while the second carried a detachment of troops, and Mason watched them twisting and swaying across the ground as they mastered the difficult terrain.

He looked farther and saw more of the strange mechanical monsters parked in a long row before the troop encampment, and at the far end of the valley there was even a small air-strip. This was Vandana's destination, and the troops below could only be Chinese.

Mason's heart began to pound and he forgot even the howling winds as he realized that he was watching a crack mountain battalion in training. The new war machines would be capable of carrying the Chinese swiftly across the high passes into Kashmir, devastating the Indian forces in their path. Here was the spearhead for the promised Chinese invasion of Ladakh, the stab aimed at India's back if she was ever again engaged by Pakistan on her western flank.

17

The Ice Gods Laugh

Mason stood for several long, unbelieving moments, bracing himself against the powerful winds that blasted across the wide valley. He rocked back and forth on his heels as he struggled to maintain his balance, and his head was bowed behind the protective shield of his upraised arm. After the first minute he had to close his streaming eyes as the tears froze to ice in his beard, and he would have paid a fortune for a pair of goggles. He kept his eyes shut for almost another minute and then opened them again, but the vast army encampment was still there, and the ungainly war machines still manoeuvred below him.

His head ached and his mind was slow to grasp all the implications of the scene. Then its full significance struck home and he realized that it was no longer of major importance that he should stop Vandana and bring her back. The vital thing was that he should return and report the presence of the Chinese and their newly developed mountain vehicles to the Indian Military Headquarters in Leh. The information that Vandana was carrying in her report would be negligible compared to the value of this new discovery, and he could no longer afford a direct confrontation which he might possibly lose.

For a moment he considered Panjit Sangh, but then he decided that he had only to lead an Indian patrol back to witness this hidden invasion force for themselves and then he would have no difficulty in convincing their Military Intelligence of the truth of the whole affair. Vandana's Land Rover was still in Leh, and should prove all the evidence he would need that he had followed her to this remote valley. Not even Chandra Singh would be able to protect her then. And in any event, he knew what course of action the young Lieutenant would want him to take. Sangh was loyal to

India and would place his country before his own neck. This poised threat already inside the frontiers of Ladakh had to be reported.

These deliberations moved slowly through his brain, too slowly, for as he stared down into the valley the crack of the rifle echoed again and a bullet kicked up a spurt of snow only a few yards behind him. He looked quickly back to the trail and saw that Vandana and her party had stopped and lowered their packs. Vandana was pointing upwards and Kalam had the rifle raised for a second shot. It was sheer bad luck that they had spotted him and Mason swore. He turned away, floundering through the snow to regain the top of the ridge and another bullet followed him. Kalam's hands were still numbed and uncertain and the shot went wide as before.

With the winds driving at his back Mason quickly reached the top of the cleft that had provided his route up, and there he stopped. He had risked his neck on the upward climb and the descent would be twice as dangerous. He faltered, shivering suddenly in the freezing wind, and then looked back. Kalam was no longer shooting and instead all four of the muffled black figures were scrambling back up the pass. They had left their packs behind and were circling back round the ice ridge in a desperate effort to head him off. He knew then that the positions had abruptly become reversed. Vandana had realized just as swiftly that his report would be of more value to the Indians than her own would be to the Chinese, and now she had definitely ordered Zakir and Kalam to chase him down and kill him. Once the hunter Mason had now become the hunted, and high in the winds the ice gods howled their screaming laughter at their own tricks of fate.

There was no time to waste. He could not descend into the valley towards the Chinese, for then he would be trapped between two fires. He had to descend the steep south wall of the ridge and get back into the pass before his enemies could cut him off. He lowered himself into the cleft, moving carefully, but an insistent note in his aching brain drilled the urgent warning that there was no time. Now that Zakir and Kalam had rid themselves of their heavy packs the race was already lost.

He slithered as fast as he dared to the foot of the cleft, grabbing at a crack in the rock that only just prevented him from pitching out into space. His heart set up a frightened clamour inside his chest, and he had to fight to impose a control on his nerves. Below him was the glassy, ten foot slope to the lower ledge and he slipped out of the cleft on his belly. His feet failed to find the holds he had stabbed out previously with the clasp knife, but he could see where he was placing his hands and he lowered himself down on the strength of his arms alone. There was a tearing agony across his shoulders, but at least he was no longer exposed to the full blast of the wind and his feet eventually touched the ledge without mishap.

He balanced there and looked down the last forty feet. There was a black, knuckled fist of rock protruding directly below, but to the left was a patch of clear snow. He hoped that it was deep, for he did not have time to climb the full distance.

He continued his descent as slowly as he dared, inching down the murderous surface. His feet were dead and his numbed hands groped with only a minimum of feeling. His face and half-bearded cheeks were frosted and lifeless. Then the inevitable happened and he slipped. He fell the last thirty feet and frantically twisted his body sideways, thrashing in mid-air as he kicked away from the face of the ridge. As much by luck as by judgement he missed the waiting fist of rock and struck into the patch of white snow. He plunged deep and it burst over him like a white sea. He drowned in snow, gasping for breath as the air was slammed from his body.

He had landed feet first, bending at the knees and turning forward in a parachutist's roll. He was buried face down and he arched his back, tucking his face beneath him so that he could breathe. The soft fall had saved him from any broken limbs and once he had recovered his breath he struggled feebly to get free. It took him five minutes to flounder back to a more solid footing, and then without hesitation he stumbled down to the trail through the pass. Without conscious thought he dragged out his revolver, pushing off the safety once more and holding it with both hands.

He did not expect to do any good with the revolver, and the most he could hope for was that the bang of the shot would keep Zakir and Kalam from pressing him too closely. However, it was not needed, for when he regained the trail his enemies were still not in sight. He hesitated, sucking the thin icy air deeply into his lungs and endeavouring to stop the trembling that had suddenly affected every muscle in his body, and then he realized that by falling half the distance down the ridge he had given himself a lead and a brief respite.

He turned away and headed back through the pass. The wind that roared through the narrow gap in the mountains was now thrusting at his back and speeding his progress, and he ran without heeding the risks of another fall. The revolver he put back on safety and returned inside his coat, for if he did any damage with it at all it would probably be by stumbling and shooting himself. Several times he glanced back but there was no sign of pursuit. He was tempted to slow down, but resisted the aching weariness of his body. He knew that Vandana would not call her two killers back, and that he needed as lengthy a start as he could get. Either Zakir and Kalam had been delayed, or after three fatiguing days in the mountains they were even less fit than he was, but whichever was the answer they would soon begin to overhaul him when he was again slowed down by Shareena.

He emerged from the pass and the winds chased him down the mountainside, almost bowling him along as he repeatedly slipped and fell. His heavy clothing protected him from any minor injuries and his luck held out against any major disasters as he continued his suicide speed. He scrambled over rocks and ploughed through crusted drifts of snow, wherever possible following what the wind had left uncovered of his previous tracks. Even then he missed the trail and would have continued blundering off course into the wilderness if Tsaro had not been watching out for his return. The guide chased after him as he passed the spot where they had separated, and grinned at him as he brought him back.

Shareena stood up and stumbled to meet them from the hollow where they had left their packs. Mason put his arm around her but for a few moments he could only gasp for breath as she plied him with anxious questions, while Tsaro stood by with his yellow-brown grin gradually turning into a puzzled frown. At last Mason was able to utter a few terse sentences of explanation and finished weakly.

"So now the situation is completely reversed. We are the ones who are being hunted and we have to get back to Leh. Kalam has a rifle which is something I didn't anticipate, and I'm no match for him with only a revolver. You'll have to tell Tsaro some tale. Tell him I've talked with his brothers' party and that now we're going back. Say that there's no longer any need for us to cross into China."

Shareena nodded uncertainly and then turned to the guide. They conversed for several minutes and Mason saw that Tsaro was clearly far from satisfied. The Ladakhi was beginning to realize that they were keeping back much of the truth and his face was wholly undecided. He argued and grumbled, but finally he turned away and picked up his pack.

Shareena said wearily, "He's taking us back. He's not happy about it but I insisted that we did not want to go on."

Mason smiled and said, "With a bit of luck he will eventually come to the conclusion that we're mad. But now we'd better get going."

He felt exhausted after the punishing activity of the past two hours, but he picked up his pack and struggled into the straps. Shareena helped him and with Tsaro leading they started on the return trek. There was very little daylight left, and Mason hoped that Zakir and Kalam had been forced to return for their own packs before settling down to any prolonged chase. They would know that they could not live after nightfall without shelter and blankets. The weather was deteriorating and the elements that had so long been their enemy might yet prove their salvation.

For an hour they marched back towards the main trail to the Karakoram Pass, and during that time there were no signs of any pursuit. Visibility grew worse and soon it was almost dark. Mason remembered suddenly that there were no stone huts away from the main trail, and for the first time he wondered how they would survive the night. He did not need Tsaro to tell him that a blizzard was blowing up and a new fear began to chill his heart. Perhaps Vandana had read the weather signs and knew that she did not need to pursue him any farther.

His fears grew as the darkness closed around them, and he knew that Shareena was also afraid. She pressed very close to him as they walked and only Tsaro seemed unconcerned. Again the constant howling of the winds was too loud to permit any worthwhile attempts at communication and they could only follow the guide as he trudged through the night. The temperature lowered and they were frozen as they walked, moving stiffly as they attempted to keep pace with the Ladakhi. How he found his way they could never know, but eventually he turned off the path and led them to a low cave that was formed beneath a mass of jumbled rocks. He gestured towards it with a casual shrug and they realized that here they were to spend the night.

The cave was four feet high and perhaps seven feet deep, but it was a blessing to crawl inside and escape from the winds. Shareena was again exhausted and Mason too was on the point of collapse. They huddled together and watched as Tsaro untied his pack and busied himself in the cave entrance. After ten minutes the Ladakhi had a small fire burning from the last of the fuel he had gathered and quickly boiled handfuls of melting snow to make more of the scalding tea that he had prepared so often before. The foul smoke from the fire was blowing back into the cave, causing them to cough and splutter, but the hot tea thawed out their stomachs and helped them slightly to revive.

Outside the approaching blizzard struck, roaring lustily in the savage night. Squalls of snow hurled past the cave mouth and great gusts of it drove inside. Beyond the white-streaked darkness there was nothing to be seen, but in the frozen mountains the tempests danced and sang, and again Mason had that peculiar feeling that the ice gods were laughing with unholy glee.

With an effort Mason shifted into a sitting position and tugged off his gloves with his teeth. He helped Shareena to restore the circulation to her hands and feet and she did the same for him. The returning blood caused them more agony than ever before, but by the time they had finished Tsaro had heated some more of their tinned meat and added biscuits to prepare a spartan meal. They ate hungrily, huddled in their blankets close to the fire which Tsaro fed sparingly with hard chips of mule dung. The smoke was drawing more tears from their eyes, but at least those tears were no longer freezing on their faces, and slowly they recovered the energy to converse. Shareena cleared her throat with a fit of coughing and asked, "Will Vandana continue to follow us, or do you think she will press on to the army camp which you saw?"

Mason said hoarsely, "I don't really know. She may have given up when she realized that I had got back across the ridge ahead of her, or she may have sent the three men back to pick up their packs and then continued to give chase. She cannot have recognized me from the distance, so she probably assumes that I'm just some stray Ladakhi who has crossed her trail by chance."

He had to keep his voice raised to sound above the roar of the storm outside, and his throat was smarting from the smoke as he continued, "There are so many factors that could affect her decision. A lot will depend upon how much loyalty she owes to the Chinese. If she was spying solely for money, then that money will be earned as soon as she delivers her report. She can collect and it won't matter to her whether the Indians receive our information or not. She will be gone before any action can be taken. On the other hand she might have genuine Communist sympathies, in which case she may do her damndest to stop us getting back."

Shareena shivered, and listened a moment to the turmoil of the storm, then she said nervously, "If she has not hurried to the army camp then perhaps the weather will solve our problems. She will die out there and her servants with her if they have not found a cave similar to this for shelter." She hesitated and finished, "I think perhaps we too will die. Tonight the temperature is lower than it has ever been before, and our fire will not burn for much longer. In this blizzard we may not survive until dawn. Then all our problems will be solved."

Mason put his arm around her and

tried hard to smile. Her eyes were terribly tired and dulled with despair and he searched for something cheerful to say. She looked up at him and her face was grey and strained beneath the dark brown skin, and he failed to find the words to reassure her. Her mouth began to tremble, her lips were slightly frost-bitten and he thought that she was about to cry.

Then abruptly the familiar crack of a rifle cut through the raging snarl of the storm. Tsaro had been sitting close beside them, watching and listening without understanding, and the bullet kicked his head back and to one side as it crashed through his left cheek. The Ladakhi tumbled backwards, his shoulders slumping against the rock wall of the cave as the bullet emptied his brains through the back of his head. He died instantly and without even a groan.

18

Duel of the Winds

The shot had been intended for Mason, but again the frozen finger on the trigger had missed its aim. Shareena screamed as Tsaro fell, staring in horror at the wrinkled yellow face with the blood-ringed hole just above the jawbone and then burying her face against Mason's coat. For a moment Mason also stared, and even with the dead guide as evidence he found it hard to believe that Vandana had been fanatical enough to follow them through the black hell of the blizzard that was now raging beyond the limits of the cave. Then instinct and training prompted his stiffened muscles into action, and grabbing Shareena he threw himself bodily sideways and dived outside into the night. He was only just in time to escape the second rifle shot that smashed into the rock wall behind him, and he realized that his enemies were either much closer or shooting much more accurately than before.

It was suicide to stay close to the flickering glow of their fire where the rifle would ultimately pick them off, and so he dragged Shareena well clear into the shrieking blackness of the blizzard. Instantly they were caught up in a blind, howling nightmare. The snow swirled around them in giant, icy flakes, whipped to a frenzy by the vicious winds, and Shareena clung against him, shaking with terror. It was impossible to calm her when every word he uttered was swept away even before it had escaped his lips, and he could not afford to have her restricting his movements with her sobbing. He gripped her shoulders and shook her hard, and then slapped his gloved hand across her face. The blow served its purpose and she became still, staring at him as they crouched face to face in the storm.

Mason leaned over her and put his mouth to her ear, lifting up the flap of her fur cap and blocking the wind with his gloved hand.

305

"Don't panic," he ordered harshly. "As yet I don't think they know that I'm armed. There's a chance if we can both keep our heads."

He couldn't know whether he was getting through to her or not, for in the pitch blackness he could no longer see her face. Then he sensed that her courage was struggling to return, and felt the movement against his hand as she nodded her head. He squeezed her shoulder hard, and then for the third time he drew Panjit Sangh's heavy army revolver and snapped off the safety catch. And this time he knew that he had to use it.

The bitter cold was cutting deep into his bones and he shivered as the winds bored through to his very soul. The refuge of the cave was still visible only a dozen yards away but he dared not return to it. He knew that Vandana and her two killers must be lurking somewhere in the freezing darkness and the final battle would have to be now, despite the utter madness of fighting in such conditions where the elements

306

could destroy them all. He still could not believe that Vandana would be so fanatical as to deliberately choose such a battleground, and then he guessed at the truth. She had been trapped by the night and the blizzard and had failed to find any alternative shelter to the one tiny cave occupied by himself and Shareena. She was now fighting only to survive, and the prize was the cave itself with its feeble hint of a warming fire.

Shareena was still now and Mason crouched beside her with the revolver in his gloved hand. It was useless to listen for an army could have marched up unheard above the thunderous snarl of the blizzard, but his eyes never wavered from the cave mouth. He prayed that Kalam would approach with the rifle, but no one emerged from the storm. He wondered then whether Vandana had realized that he was armed, perhaps she had seen the revolver in his hand as he had approached her in the pass. Either way she was taking no chances, and he was faced with the choice of continuing to outwait them, or attempting to find them in the night.

His hands were rapidly becoming numb once more, and that helped him to reach his decision. If he sat and waited he would only freeze, where by carrying the battle forward he would at least circulate his bloodstream, and perhaps give himself the edge for the final encounter. He chose to attack.

His biggest worry was Shareena. If he left her then it was possible that Zakir or Kalam would find her alone, or that she would be lost out of sight of the cave and that no one would ever find her again. Either way she would be dead, and the only satisfactory solution was to take her with him. He pushed his mouth close to her ear again and shouted beneath the cover of his hand.

"I'm going after them. Try not to hinder me, but stay close and keep a tight grip on my coat. Understand?"

Again he felt her nod, and again he squeezed her shoulder. He felt her take a hold upon the flapping corner of his coat, and then he began to lead her farther away from the cave. He had roughly marked the direction from which the last shot had come, and knew that he had to circle to his left. The wind was freezing his face and the snow was heavy upon his shoulders as he crawled across the icy earth, and his teeth were clenched tightly together. He could see nothing but the falling white flakes that rushed swiftly past in front of his face.

He glanced back repeatedly at the cave, partly because they would be completely lost if they did not keep in sight of that feeble flicker of firelight, and partly because he hoped that Vandana would yet make the mistake of thinking that he had fled and lead her companions into the tiny shelter. There was a limit to how long she could play a waiting game, for she too must be rapidly freezing in the sub-zero night.

Mercifully his head had cleared a little, either through necessity or because he was at last becoming accustomed to the altitude and the thin air. He stopped, crouching, and rested the revolver in his lap while he pounded his hands together to keep them alive. The clapping sound was wholly drowned by the winds that seemed to be fighting their own violent duel around him, and he knew that he had to keep his right hand flexible enough to handle the gun. When his hand tingled he fitted the revolver back into his gloved palm, and continued his painful, crawling search.

Shareena crawled beside him, hanging slightly back and keeping her right hand locked around a fold of his coat. She was already frozen and moved mechanically whenever the coat tugged her along. She had neither fear nor courage now, her mind and her nerves were blunted beyond endurance, and it no longer mattered what happened to her. She could not even think clearly enough to pray that the outcome would be settled swiftly. Her face was bowed against her chest and her eyes were closed, she felt nothing but the agonising cold, and heard nothing but the shrieking of the blizzard.

Mason knew that she was more dead than alive, but there was nothing that he could do for her. There was nothing that he could do for either of them except to find Kalam and the rifle. Then they could return to the safety of the cave.

A stab of alarm made him look round and he suddenly realized that there was nothing but the hideous night. He had strayed too far and the cave was swamped by darkness. He turned and crawled hastily back, scrambling through snow and over icy earth. He all but dropped the precious revolver and crashed his shoulder and then his knee against unseen rocks. He could feel the weight of Shareena dragging behind him and fresh snow blasted into his eyes. The winds duelled and the ice gods roared with drunken, boisterous laughter. He had an awful fear that the tiny fire had gone out and that he would never find the cave again, but then the driving snow cleared for a moment and he saw the faint glow of red.

He halted and Shareena huddled close beside him. The panic began to fade, and slowly his brain became clear again. He inched closer to the cave, enough to see that it was still empty, and then he drew back. A savage grin slowly cracked

311

the mask of ice that had frozen to his beard, and his nerves came back under control. His own panic had told him where he would find Vandana. She and her companions had to be close, very close, close enough in fact to be watching the cave mouth. They too would not dare to lose sight of their only hope of shelter, and must still be waiting for him to return. He had only to move along the outer edge of the circle from which the red glimmer of the fire was visible, and somewhere along the line he must find them. Perhaps they were waiting for him to do exactly that, but even so he preferred to carry the battle forward.

His hands had become numbed once more, and for the second time he rested the revolver in his lap while he massaged them back into some small semblance of life. Then he backed away until he could only just see the glow of the fire, pushing the helpless Shareena behind him. He turned and began to circle once more, crouching low on the frozen mountainside, but this time he ensured that he strayed neither towards nor away from that comforting flicker of red.

In these blind, groping conditions he knew that he would have very little warning of when he had found his quarry, and most likely the first knowledge he would have of their presence would be when one of them bumped bodily against him. The thought kept him constantly prepared as he fumbled his way forward, and his eyes were narrowed to aching slits as he tried to penetrate the snowfilled darkness. More rocks and obstacles passed beneath him, banging at his knees and catching at his clothes. He crawled into a snowdrift that bogged him down for several frightening seconds, and then he had to detour to pass by a barrier of rocks which he encountered with his left hand. Shareena was a dead weight that he towed behind him, and he knew that if her fingers had not stiffened around his coat tail she would have dropped behind. Her grip was now frozen fast.

It was twenty minutes since Tsaro had been shot dead, and again the encounter came abruptly. There was a fleeting instant in which a human shadow loomed above him, visible only in that it momentarily obscured the white streaks of driving snow, and then a strangling scarf lashed forward to coil at his neck. Mason had looked up, but tonight there was no guiding moonlight, and the shrieking winds chose to intervene. The deadly kiss of Khali found its mark even in the stormy darkness, but the weighted end of the scarf was plucked away before it could properly coil around its victim's throat. The strangler jerked, but the scarf pulled free without snapping Mason's neck. Mason lifted his revolver and fired. It could have been either Zakir or Kalam who had attacked him, but some strange insight made him visualize an agonized starved face as the dark murderer screamed and spun away.

There was an echoing scream as the falling man vanished into the night. It came from behind and was unmistakably uttered by Shareena. Mason twisted round clumsily and sensed rather than saw the second dark figure who straddled over the kneeling girl, tightening another of the evil silk scarves around her throat.

Again Mason fired, pressing closer and seeing the vague shape twist and stagger in the gloom. He was on his feet now and instinct told him that the second strangler had only been lightly hit. His gloved finger had slipped from the trigger and he had to fumble with the revolver with both hands to keep it level. He found the trigger again and fired a third shot, and then a fourth. One of the bullets scored a hit and the second of their enemies went down.

Mason stood panting, and then he dragged Shareena up beside him. The blizzard continued to rage unabated, and he carefully pushed both bodies with his foot. They were both dead weights and he knew he had killed Zakir and Kalam. He wondered for a moment why they had chosen to attack him with the strangling scarves, even though the scarves were ideal for close quarters and obviously their favourite weapons. The answer came almost immediately. Vandana had the rifle.

His first thought was to change his position, for the revolver shots had marked him down. Then he realized that neither of them could continue to play blind games of hide and seek in the storm-filled night, and so he held his ground. If she had been certain of his position she would have fired at him by now. The fact that she had not used the rifle meant that the distorting winds were confusing her hearing, and that she would have to come closer to find him. His heart was thudding painfully but he waited.

Minutes passed, and then some sixth sense caused him to look towards the cave. A muffled figure was moving slowly into the dim firelight, and he saw the barrel of the rifle glint in a brief play of flame. He steadied the revolver, but some deep, subconscious reluctance stayed his fire. The rifle was no threat and its owner was clearly beaten. She slumped with her shoulders against the rock wall, almost falling, and he moved warily towards her.

Her mouth was open, but he could not hear what she said. The words were flicked away by the pitiless winds. Then she raised the rifle with both hands, holding it out and then thrusting it feebly away into the night. It was total surrender but Mason hesitated, wondering what had happened to her guide.

He did not trust her, but neither could he shoot her down in cold blood. He watched her for a moment, still hesitating, but then the lifeless weight of Shareena leaning against him told him that he had to return to the shelter of the cave. The girl had lost consciousness and if they stayed out in the open any longer she would freeze to death. Mason wrapped his left arm around her waist, and still levelling the revolver he stumbled slowly towards the cave.

19

White Nightmare

Vandana watched as Mason emerged from the blizzard. She leaned back against the rock beside the cave mouth with her arms hanging limply at her sides, and he could see that she was struggling to breathe. The altitude had beaten her as much as the storm. She wore furs, but her face was almost blue with cold and frostbite, and her eyes were raw and bloodshot. Mason felt no exceptional pity for her, for he knew that he and Shareena presented very much the same picture.

As he approached over the last yard she seemed to collapse and slide down the rock face, turning so that she fell into the cave. Mason stiffened, still alert for the missing guide, but nothing happened. He could take no more of the foul arctic night, and still supporting Shareena he stumbled the last few feet and lowered her into the cave. He crawled in beside her and dragged her deeper into the shelter. The fire was almost dead and with frozen fingers he piled it up with the last few chips of fuel. He dropped the revolver as he worked, for his body craved warmth and for the moment nothing else was important.

Vandana crawled closer to the blaze and huddled beside it face down. Her furs began to steam but Mason ignored her. Shareena was still unconscious and he turned his attention to the girl, brushing the piled snow from her clothing and covering her with their blankets. The cave was cramped and there was no room to work beside the dead body of Tsaro, and so he hauled the guide out into the darkness. His body cringed as it was once again slashed and pummelled by the winds, and he quickly returned to the cave.

He performed the seemingly endless task of removing Shareena's gloves and boots and vigorously rubbing her hands and feet. Her limbs might have been made of glass or marble, but gradually

319

he brought them back to life. Shareena moaned softly with the pain but she did not recover consciousness. He replaced her boots and gloves and straightened the blankets over her, and then sat back wearily on his heels. He was almost beyond the point of exhaustion and ready to fall down and sleep beside her, but slowly he became aware that he was being watched. He turned his head and looked into Vandana's eyes.

Her mouth opened and moved, and then the smoke from the fire racked her body with coughing. She tried again and said weakly, "Paul, somehow I knew it would be you. I knew when I saw you standing above the ridge. No ordinary man would have attempted that climb to head us off."

Mason hesitated without answering, and then asked harshly, "What happened to your guide?"

She looked away, lowering her head.

"Kalam killed him. He became too curious — asked too many questions, about you and the army camp in the valley."

"On your orders."

"No, this time he did not wait for orders."

She looked up into his face, but he did not believe her. She waited for him to speak and for a long moment there was silence. Then she looked at the revolver.

"Kalam and Zakir are dead."

It was a statement, and not a question. He nodded.

"Everybody's dead. There's just the three of us. You, myself, and Shareena."

She nodded. "I guessed you would be armed. That was why I sent them to look for you before I approached the cave."

She shivered, and suddenly her teeth were chattering uncontrollably, as though her lower jaw was banging and rattling on a loose hinge. It was a horrible sound, grating on Mason's nerves even worse than the fearsome roaring of the elements. She began to cry and her eyes begged through her tears.

"Paul, p-please. I'm frozen. My f-feet are frozen."

Mason hesitated, but there was a desperate agony in her appeal that he could not deny. He crawled round the fire towards her and pulled off her boots, and then worked hard to restore her circulation as he had already done for Shareena. He succeeded and derived a vicious sense of pleasure from the excruciating pain he caused her as her blood began to flow once more to her ice-like toes. He was saving her feet from frostbite, but at least he was making her suffer.

He did the same for her hands, and the activity was as beneficial for himself as it was for her. Afterwards he raided Tsaro's pack, and while there was still a fire he boiled up more snow to make scalding tea for them both. He tried to revive Shareena but had no success, so it was impossible to give her a drink also.

Outside the night was now a grey-white maelstrom of thickly falling snow. The winds still howled through the mountains and the temperature had dropped like a falling stone. The dark side of the moon could have been no worse, and Mason knew that the odds were still high that they would all be dead by morning. The fire was almost out and there was no more fuel.

They could no longer afford to be enemies and he realized that he had no need to fear any treachery from Vandana. They needed each other to survive. He left her and went out into the night to strip the dead corpse of Tsaro of its thick woollen coat, but he did not risk losing himself in an attempt to find the bodies of Zakir and Kalam. He returned to the cave and made a bed of the coat and the dead man's blanket, and then laid Shareena upon it. He took off her heavy top coat and his own and made Vandana do likewise. Then he ordered Vandana to lay close beside the girl and covered them up with the spare coats and blankets. Finally he slipped in beside them with Shareena in the middle and they huddled together so that their body heat would help to keep each other alive. He could do no more, and could only pray that he had done enough.

* * *

They lived. Sheer exhaustion buried Mason in a helpless sleep but eventually he awoke. The blizzard had passed, but it had built up a drift of snow that all but blocked the entrance to the cave. A jagged but clear patch of daylight showed in one corner, and although the winds still moaned and blew they had slackened in their senseless fury.

Mason lay with his arms wrapped around Shareena and the girl was warm against him. A faint movement told him that she too was alive and he felt a slow rise of relief. He was reluctant to move, and then abruptly a spasm of alarm shot through him. It passed immediately as he realized that his revolver was still by his side, while Vandana lay harmlessly asleep. She too had her arms around Shareena, and all three of them were locked close together.

He lay quiet for a while, not thinking, but simply drawing in the rare luxury of feeling warm. Then he realized that his feet were outside that radius of body-warmth, and that again they were without feeling. He separated himself with difficulty from Shareena's embrace, but still neither of the women awoke as he got out from under the blankets. He pulled on his top coat and with his back bowed moved to the entrance. The drift of snow that had covered the cave mouth had helped to shut out the freezing winds and saved their lives, but now it took him half an hour to dig a path out with his hands.

When he turned back Vandana was awake. He picked up his revolver and pushed it safely inside his coat, but despite the precaution he sensed that she would still offer no danger. They would continue to need each other all the way back to civilization, and only then would she become an enemy again.

She said quietly, "We are going back?"

He nodded. "Back to Leh."

"The Chinese are closer. They need my report, and I could protect you."

He shook his head.

"I thought not." She looked away and then said simply, "We must wake your little friend. I think she will need medical attention, and if we do not start now while the weather is favourable we may never escape from this awful land."

Mason agreed and together they worked gently on Shareena to bring her back to consciousness. When the girl awoke her eyes were dull and not quite comprehending, and they had to help her to put on her heavy coat. Mason rolled up the blankets and Tsaro's long coat into two bundles. One he gave to Vandana and the other he carried himself, together with his pack into which he crammed as much of the remaining supplies as possible. Then unwillingly they left the snug comfort of the cave to face the long march back to Leh.

The mountainside was now thickly blanketed in snow, and the bodies of Zakir, Kalam and Tsaro had been buried as though they had never existed. The winds still beat up storming snow flurries but there were no flakes actually falling. The bleak, frozen peaks stood out sharply against a thin blue sky. It was a lost land, bitter and empty.

The three walked slowly, in a close group with Shareena between them. It was more difficult than walking in single file, but the girl was not fully capable of moving without support. The snow had blotted out the path that Tsaro had followed, but Mason's sense of direction was good and after several hours they stumbled back on to the main trail. They made many stops, wherever there was enough shelter to escape the winds, and their progress was limping and painful. Many times they had to struggle out of deep drifts and the journey became a white nightmare.

If the weather had not been as lenient as was possible they would not have survived, but after the ferocity of the previous night the winds had strangely calmed, as though they too were spent and exhausted. Without a guide Mason walked in the constant fear that he would lose them all in the arctic wilderness, and he felt a great sense of relief when they regained the main trade route. From here the way was more clearly marked, both by the occasional stone huts and the many cairns of stones built up by passing pilgrims, and even if the weather deteriorated again he felt that they could lay up in one of the huts and still find their way. They turned their backs on the Karakoram Pass, still several days march away in the distant north, and headed back towards Leh.

They reached the first hut shortly after mid-afternoon, and here they stopped because Mason could not remember whether there was another hut that they could safely reach before nightfall. He had been less successful than Tsaro in finding fuel for a fire, and so they ate cold food. It was already winter and soon the passes would be completely blocked, and he guessed that it was many weeks since a mule train had last travelled the trail. Tsaro had already gathered what few droppings had been available for fuel. A paraffin stove would now have been a godsend, and Mason wished that there had been time to fit out more fully for this wild expedition before the start.

As night closed in they again removed their top coats and used them as additional blankets, sleeping close together in a warm, life-sustaining huddle. Only by keeping each other alive could they hope to survive, and they were all fully aware of that one vital fact. The bitter cold never for one moment allowed them to forget. Shareena was again given the warmest place in the middle, and at dawn she was at least no worse than she had been at the beginning of the first day.

The outward trip had taken three days, but the return journey lasted five. They were five, freezing, nightmarish days in which only Mason's dogged refusal to lay down and die kept them slowly moving. Another blizzard would have brought about a swift and final end, but although the winds continued to prove their most hostile enemy they mercifully failed to build up into blizzard force. Because of Shareena they had to rest often, and after the first two days Vandana was also relying heavily upon Mason for support. They had no strength for conversation and barely exchanged a dozen words during the whole of those five killing days, and Shareena did not speak at all.

There were fresh falls of snow during

each of the first three nights, so that each morning six or seven inches of it covered the trail. Where it had drifted they had to fight their way through, and in one narrow pass it took them almost two hours to cover a hundred yards. The altitude was again affecting them badly, starving their lungs of oxygen, and they were never free from throbbing headaches. They were fortunate to find a hut for each night, sometimes stopping while there remained several hours of daylight rather than risk being stranded without shelter, and each night they slept the exhausted sleep of the near-dead.

Finally, late on the fifth afternoon, they stumbled out of the mountain pass above Leh, and saw the old town with its high-walled replica of the Potala Palace lying on the plain below. They had survived, and the white nightmare was over.

★ ★ ★

Mason dumped his pack as soon as he realized that it was no longer needed, and so he was able to devote what remained of his strength to helping the two women over the last mile. It was dark when they descended from the mountains, and they succeeded in entering the town without attracting any undue attentions. Mason used the roundabout back route which Tsaro had showed him on the way out, and his first move was to head for a doctor's surgery which he remembered from his search of the bazaars.

The doctor proved to be a small, disgruntled Hindu wearing a white coat and spectacles, but his manner thawed when he realized that Mason had money to pay for treatment. He was curious and suspicious, and regarded them dubiously once he had invited them inside. He looked from one to the other, but Mason gave him no time to ask questions, and while Vandana stood aside they carried Shareena into the surgery. The girl was suffering badly from exposure and fatigue, and Mason helped to remove her outer clothing before he was sent outside.

Vandana had entered the surgery, but she turned and preceded him into the waiting-room. They stood awkwardly while the doctor attended to Shareena behind the closed door, and something in her stance told Mason that the truce was over and that again they were enemies. She leaned against the wall, closing her eyes for a moment, and then she opened them to look into his face. She said wearily, "Well, Paul. We have succeeded. This is Leh, and we are alive. What do you propose to do with me now?"

Mason said, "As soon as the doctor has looked after Shareena I'll get him to examine you, and give you any treatment you need. After that I'll ask him to call the military authorities and have them come to fetch us. I won't enjoy doing it, but I shall have to hand you over."

She breathed deeply, but her red-rimmed eyes did not leave his face.

"You could let me go. After what we have endured together you owe me that. Without me you might have saved yourself, but you would not have saved your little friend."

"Let you go," he repeated. "To take

your report to the Chinese. To betray India?"

"To betray India!" Suddenly and hysterically she laughed. "To betray India? Paul, what do you know of India? What do you know of the starving millions of India, of the famines and the poverty that the politicians will not even admit exists? What do you know of the corruption and bribery that is rife in every government and political circle in India? Paul, you know nothing of India. Here Democracy has utterly failed, and Communism is the only hope that India has for the future."

"You believe that? And because of it you've sold your country to the Chinese?"

"To Communism, Paul. And if it has to be Chinese Communism then perhaps that is another tragedy, but anything is better than the situation that now exists. There are more Indians dying now in the famine areas of Bihar than will ever die in fighting the Chinese invasion of Ladakh."

He stared, suddenly wanting to believe that she was sincere, and then said harshly, "You talk of famine, but those jewels you wore in Srinagar would feed a thousand."

She nodded. "But for how long, Paul? And what is a thousand amongst millions. All of the endless streams of foreign aid that have flowed into India from Britain and America have failed to solve the problem. It has mostly flowed into the pockets of the politicians. It is the system of government that must be changed, and the only workable alternative is Communism."

Mason hesitated, and then said slowly, "Perhaps you are right, but not the blind, hating, deluding Communism of Chairman Mao Tse Tung. Not that! I'm sorry, Vandana, but nothing will induce me to let you take your report to the Chinese."

"Nothing?"

Her face was hard and her gloved hand slowly moved. Steel glittered in the light of the electric lamp above them, and for the first time he saw what she had kept concealed. The scalpel had a blued, razor edge, and he realized that she must have picked it up from the surgery while he was helping the doctor with Shareena. She was breathing hard now, but although her voice was strained and weak it remained level.

"Paul, I too am sorry. But I will not be handed over to the Indian police. I will not be taken tamely back to Srinagar to be executed as a spy. Perhaps you are strong enough to take this knife away, but you will have to kill me to do so. Otherwise I shall kill you. I prefer to end this business now."

He faced her, but did not move. There was a moment of tight silence, broken only by their breathing, and then she came away from the wall. The scalpel was held ready in her gloved hand, and her bloodshot eyes burned in her wind-raw face. Mason hesitated, and backed away. He knew that he could take her, but not without the risk of killing her.

She saw him retreat, and hesitated in turn. She said hoarsely, "Another truce, Paul. My report will be of limited value once you have reported the whereabouts of the advance force camped in the valley beyond the passes. The two will cancel each other out and the situation will not be much changed. We can afford that and withdraw with honour. This way one of us must die."

Mason wavered, and for a moment he remembered her brown body spread naked upon the golden sari on their island in the lake. He thought of the Kama Sutra and their hour of love-making together. Insurance, said the cold, professional part of his brain; simple, feminine insurance to weaken him in such a situation as the present. Yet he knew it was not wholly so. He could not kill her, and suddenly he knew that neither could he hand her over to the Indians for execution.

He said slowly, "I will make a bargain. But not yours. I came to India to help Lieutenant Sangh, and I want to ensure that he gets his liberty. To be one hundred per cent sure of doing that I first have to nail down Chandra Singh. I have less taste for a traitor than I have for a woman of fortune, and I'd rather eliminate the Sikh than you. Help me to

336

do that and I'll grant you your life and freedom."

Vandana stared at him, trying hard to grasp his proposition. And then she lowered the scalpel and nodded. In the same moment something seemed to break inside her and she fell against him sobbing.

20

A Man of Honour

After a day of complete rest in the small guest-house hotel Mason and Vandana drove back to Srinagar in Shareena's Land Rover. They had left the girl behind in the care of the doctor, whom Mason had persuaded to keep quiet about her presence for the next two days. She was very ill after their ordeal in the mountains, but the doctor had assured them that she would recover. Mason had been reluctant to leave her behind, but he was confident that when he ultimately approached the Indian authorities the army would be grateful enough to bring her directly back to Srinagar by air. It would save her from the rigours of the two day drive, which she was not fit to face.

They covered the journey sanely, with no rush and an overnight stop at Kargil.

At first Mason was still just a little distrustful of his companion, but now that Vandana had chosen to co-operate she made no attempt to break their truce. On the easier stretches she relieved him at the wheel, and although they drove mostly in silence she was not unfriendly. On the afternoon of the second day they passed through the massive gateway of the Zoji La, and both were glad to leave the high plateau of Ladakh behind them as they descended into the more gentle vale of Kashmir.

They entered Srinagar at dusk, when a gentle breeze was just beginning to ripple the placid surface of the Dal Lake. It was too late for the plans that Mason had in mind, and after a necessary stop for a meal they went directly to the *Shalimar*. They spent the night on the houseboat, sharing Vandana's bed but only for sleep. They were both very tired.

The next morning they visited the offices of Air India, and were fortunate to find that the airline had a flight to Amritsar that same day. The departure time was two p.m. and they booked for

Vandana a one-way through ticket to New Delhi. Where she would go from there was her own affair, she did not say, and Mason did not ask.

They returned to the houseboat, and on the way Vandana kept her part of the bargain and made a telephone call to Chandra Singh. Mason stood beside her as she informed the Sikh that she had been obliged to come back to Srinagar and that she needed to see him urgently. She spoke in a calm, toneless voice, and replaced the receiver before he could ask any questions. Mason smiled with quiet satisfaction.

Aboard the *Shalimar* there was nothing to do but wait, but Mason had no doubt that the Sikh would come. Vandana was silent and her face wore no expression. Once or twice she glanced at her wristwatch, but apart from that she sat motionless on the low divan in the larger cabin. They had cleared the dust covers from the furniture, but the cabin still lacked its previous exotic air.

Mason stayed on deck until he saw the army jeep pull to a stop on the

340

road that ran along the edge of the lake, then he quietly re-entered the cabin. Vandana looked at him for a moment and he nodded. Five minutes passed, and then they heard the sound of a *shikara* bumping against the side of the houseboat. They had left the cabin door open, and a moment later the bulky figure of Chandra Singh was framed in the doorway. He was out of uniform and again wearing his dark suit and the dark blue turban. His beard was still neatly contained in the little chin-strap hairnet, and his heavy round face was troubled.

He hesitated before stepping into the gloom of the cabin, and then his searching eyes saw Vandana sitting silently on the divan. He said curtly, "Miss Vandana, why are you here. By now you should be safely in China. You will endanger — "

He stopped. Vandana had turned away and would not look at him, and for the first time he saw Mason farther back in the cabin. There were no chairs, and so Mason sat cross-legged on a cushion with a low table before him. He said coldly, "Vandana has nothing to say to you,

Major. You have to deal with me."

The Sikh stared, and then came into the cabin. His step was quick and purposeful, but faltered when he saw the heavy army revolver that lay upon the table between Mason's casually resting hands. He stopped again, his dark eyes wary, seeking an answer from Vandana but finding none.

"Sit down."

The order forced his attention back to Mason. The revolver still lay harmlessly on the table, but he knew better than to try and reach for it, or to reach for any weapon of his own. A cushion had been placed for him, and slowly he lowered his huge bulk down, crossing his legs as he faced Mason across the table. He had not panicked and his normally harsh voice was unchanged.

"You are a fool, Mister Mason. There is still a warrant out for your arrest for your part in the activities of the traitor Panjit Sangh and the Pakistani spy Lalshar Shafi. What do you hope to gain by this?"

Mason smiled. "But you are not a fool,

Major. Neither are you blind. You can see that I have succeeded in bringing Vandana back to Srinagar. Her two servants are dead and I had to save her life during a blizzard in Ladakh, because of this she is now willing to testify to the truth of this whole affair. I can now prove conclusively that Shafi's little games were irrelevant compared to the scale of the Chinese activities in this area. I can prove that Lieutenant Sangh is the victim of a complicated plot, and that he has been unjustly accused so that the true enemies of India can continue their work undisturbed. I have some very interesting information for the Indian Army concerning an advance invasion force of Chinese troops already encamped in a hidden valley inside the borders of Ladakh, plus details of some ingenious new machines they have developed for transporting those troops and their equipment across the lesser known passes where they can make a surprise attack. And finally I can also prove the identity of the one real traitor operating in the higher levels of Indian

Military Intelligence."

Chandra Singh had listened without any change of expression, but beneath the black-bearded mask of his face he had become hard and tensed. Mason could detect the betraying stiffness in the way he sat, and he too was sharply alert. The big Sikh gazed into his eyes for a few moments, and then again he looked towards Vandana. She had been watching and listening but quickly turned her head once more. Chandra Singh hesitated, but decided against speaking to her. He knew that she would not answer. His head came back slowly and his eyes bored out from under the folds of the dark blue turban. His voice had softened as he asked, "Why do you tell all this to me? If you know so much then what is the purpose of this meeting? What do you want me to do?"

His tone was not defeat, but acceptance of the facts. Mason answered bluntly.

"To me it does not matter what you choose to do. I intend to make a written report of everything I know. It will take me approximately an hour to complete that report, and then I shall officially place it before the Military authorities here in Srinagar. There is nothing you can do that will alter that."

"I see."

Chandra Singh stared at him for another moment, and then looked down at the revolver that lay on the table between them. He seemed to deliberate within himself, and then turned yet again to look towards Vandana. He stared for several moments at the back of her head, as though striving to will his one-time accomplice into facing him. It was a silent battle of mental telepathy, a clash of minds which Vandana seemed to sense but choose not to obey. Chandra Singh sighed heavily, and his eyes moved back to Mason. He placed his hands upon the table, very close to the revolver, and slowly pushed himself upright. He said quietly, "Then I will leave you to write your report. I suggest that you hand it to Captain Dayal Sen. He is the correct man to approach."

Mason had watched him every inch of the way, and as the big man turned to leave he said softly.

"Major Singh, you are a Sikh I believe."

It was a remark that needed no answer, but Chandra Singh turned back and again their eyes met.

Mason looked up at him and continued calmly. "The Sikhs are a noble race, they are jealous of their honour. Every Sikh is a courageous fighting man, and it is a known fact that they form the backbone of the Indian Army. The very name Singh means Lion and it applies to the whole race. I have been told that even in a country which is noted for its poverty and its beggars, there has never been a Sikh beggar. The Sikhs are too proud to beg." He paused and then asked: "Has there ever been a Sikh traitor?"

Chandra Singh was silent for a moment, but he stood tall and straight. His expression did not change and his eyes did not falter from Mason's gaze. Then he smiled faintly, and almost sadly, and said, "I understand you, Mister Mason. And it seems that you also understand a Sikh. I thank you for the hour."

He turned away for the second time, and without sparing another glance for Vandana he walked stiffly out of the cabin. They heard him climb down into his waiting *shikara*, and then there was the faint splash of water as the boatman poled him away. Mason arose and went to Vandana, but when his hand rested on her shoulder she bitterly pushed him away.

★ ★ ★

An hour later Mason and Vandana stood together at the airport, waiting while the last minutes before the departure time of her flight to Amritsar ticked slowly away. Vandana had recovered her composure, she was again wearing a selection of her jewels, and despite the lines of strain around her eyes she was again looking exceptionally beautiful. She wore her red sari and a white shawl. She looked at Mason and asked, "What will happen if Chandra Singh does not do as you expect?"

Mason shrugged. "If he decides to fight

and deny my charges then the whole thing will take longer to settle. It will not be so easy for me but the end will be the same. However, I don't think he will destroy what is left of his honour as a Sikh with all the additional publicity of an enquiry and a trial. Your presence at our interview should have been enough to convince him that he is finished, and I don't think your actual testimony will be needed. Either way our bargain still stands, and you are free to leave."

"And what will you do? Where will you go?"

He shrugged again, smiling wryly. "My holiday is over. I have to return to my job in Hong Kong. But first I'll hang around Srinagar until Shareena has been flown down from Leh, and until Panjit Sangh has definitely been released."

Vandana smiled almost as wryly. "Lieutenant Sangh chooses his friends wisely. I wish I had known."

As they talked her aircraft had landed, and now it was ready to leave. She hesitated, and then held out her jewelled hand.

"Goodbye, Paul."

"Goodbye, Vandana."

He held her hand for a moment, and then raised it. His mission was over and he could afford to relax and play the casual dandy. The hand sparkled, but between the golden chains that linked her rings and her bracelet there was room to touch a gallant kiss. She drew away and shook her head.

"Please, Paul. You cannot fool me any more. I know there is another man beneath the idle galahad who kisses my hand. Or perhaps you are two men. I cannot be sure."

She hesitated, and then turned away, walking slowly out to the waiting plane. Mason watched her go, and wondered whether perhaps she was two women. The ruthless one, and the woman he had known for only an hour on their lovers' island. She did not look back, and five minutes later her plane took flight and vanished in the blue sky to the south.

★ ★ ★

Mason took a taxi to the army camp, and was delayed for ten minutes in the guardroom at the gate before he succeeded in gaining an interview with Captain Dayal Sen. A two-man escort, one corporal and one soldier, led him to the headquarters of the Military Police, marching stiffly one on either side. He was admitted into a large office where the ferret-faced policeman was working behind a littered desk, and after Sen had studied him for a moment the escort were ordered to wait outside the closed door.

Dayal Sen leaned back and offered him a chair, when Mason was seated he said curiously, "So you are the mysterious Mister Paul Mason. This is indeed a surprise. I believed that you had either fled Srinagar, or been drowned in the Jhelum."

Mason said quietly, "Didn't Major Singh warn you to expect me?"

Dayal Sen became rigid, his sharp eyes suddenly alert.

"What do you know of Major Singh?"

"I spoke to him a little over an hour ago. I told him that I would shortly be presenting you with new facts and information which would prove the innocence of Lieutenant Panjit Sangh." He paused. "You are staring hard, Captain. Has anything happened to the Major?"

Dayal Sen continued to stare for several long minutes, and then he said slowly, "Exactly one hour ago Major Chandra Singh returned to his office in this building. He tidied his papers, signed some reports, and then sat behind his desk and took his own life by blowing out his brains with a pistol."

"Did he leave any message?"

"No, there was no message. No note of any kind."

Mason closed his eyes for a moment. It was over, and he felt suddenly old and drained and tired. When he looked up he said wearily:

"There was no need. I can explain . . . "

A FOOT IN THE GRAVE
Bruce Marshall

About to be imprisoned and tortured in Buenos Aires, John Smith escapes, only to become involved in an aeroplane hijacking.

DEAD TROUBLE
Martin Carroll

Trespassing brought Jennifer Denning more than she bargained for. She was totally unprepared for the violence which was to lie in her path.

HOURS TO KILL
Ursula Curtiss

Margaret went to New Mexico to look after her sick sister's rented house and felt a sharp edge of fear when the absent landlady arrived.

THE DEATH OF ABBE DIDIER
Richard Grayson

Inspector Gautier of the Sûreté investigates three crimes which are strangely connected.

NIGHTMARE TIME
Hugh Pentecost

Have the missing major and his wife met with foul play somewhere in the Beaumont Hotel, or is their disappearance a carefully planned step in an act of treason?

BLOOD WILL OUT
Margaret Carr

Why was the manor house so oddly familiar to Elinor Howard? Who would have guessed that a Sunday School outing could lead to murder?

THE DRACULA MURDERS
Philip Daniels

The Horror Ball was interrupted by a spectral figure who warned the merrymakers they were tampering with the unknown.

THE LADIES
OF LAMBTON GREEN
Liza Shepherd

Why did murdered Robin Colquhoun's picture pose such a threat to the ladies of Lambton Green?

CARNABY
AND THE GAOLBREAKERS
Peter N. Walker

Detective Sergeant James Aloysius Carnaby-King is sent to prison as bait. When he joins in an escape he is thrown headfirst into a vicious murder hunt.

MUD IN HIS EYE
Gerald Hammond

The harbourmaster's body is found mangled beneath Major Smyle's yacht. What is the sinister significance of the illicit oysters?

THE SCAVENGERS
Bill Knox

Among the masses of struggling fish in the *Tecta*'s nets was a larger, darker, ominously motionless form . . . the body of a skin diver.

DEATH IN ARCADY
Stella Phillips

Detective Inspector Matthew Furnival works unofficially with the local police when a brutal murder takes place in a caravan camp.

STORM CENTRE
Douglas Clark

Detective Chief Superintendent Masters, temporarily lecturing in a police staff college, finds there's more to the job than a few weeks relaxation in a rural setting.

THE MANUSCRIPT MURDERS
Roy Harley Lewis

Antiquarian bookseller Matthew Coll, acquires a rare 16th century manuscript. But when the Dutch professor who had discovered the journal is murdered, Coll begins to doubt its authenticity.

SHARENDEL
Margaret Carr

Ruth didn't want all that money. And she didn't want Aunt Cass to die. But at Sharendel things looked different. She began to wonder if she had a split personality.

MURDER TO BURN
Laurie Mantell

Sergeants Steven Arrow and Lance Brendon, of the New Zealand police force, come upon a woman's body in the water. When the dead woman is identified they begin to realise that they are investigating a complex fraud.

YOU CAN HELP ME
Maisie Birmingham

Whilst running the Citizens' Advice Bureau, Kate Weatherley is attacked with no apparent motive. Then the body of one of her clients is found in her room.

DAGGERS DRAWN
Margaret Carr

Stacey Manston was the kind of girl who could take most things in her stride, but three murders were something different . . .

THE MONTMARTRE MURDERS
Richard Grayson

Inspector Gautier of Sûreté investigates the disappearance of artist Théo, the heir to a fortune.

GRIZZLY TRAIL
Gwen Moffat

Miss Pink, alone in the Rockies, helps in a search for missing hikers, solves two cruel murders and has the most terrifying experience of her life when she meets a grizzly bear!

BLINDMAN'S BLUFF
Margaret Carr

Kate Deverill had considered suicide. It was one way out — and preferable to being murdered.

BEGOTTEN MURDER
Martin Carroll

When Susan Phillips joined her aunt on a voyage of 12,000 miles from her home in Melbourne, she little knew their arrival would germinate the seeds of murder planted long ago.

WHO'S THE TARGET?
Margaret Carr

Three people whom Abby could identify as her parents' murderers wanted her dead, but she decided that maybe Jason could have been the target.

THE LOOSE SCREW
Gerald Hammond

After a motor smash, Beau Pepys and his cousin Jacqueline, her fiancé and dotty mother, suspect that someone had prearranged the death of their friend. But who, and why?

CASE WITH THREE HUSBANDS
Margaret Erskine

Was it a ghost of one of Rose Bonner's late husbands that gave her old Aunt Agatha such a terrible shock and then murdered her in her bed?

THE END OF THE RUNNING
Alan Evans

Lang continued to push the men and children on and on. Behind them were the men who were hunting them down, waiting for the first signs of exhaustion before they pounced.

CARNABY AND THE HIJACKERS
Peter N. Walker

When Commander Pigeon assigns Detective Sergeant Carnaby-King to prevent a raid on a bullion-carrying passenger train, he knows that there are traitors in high positions.

TREAD WARILY AT MIDNIGHT
Margaret Carr

If Joanna Morse hadn't been so hasty she wouldn't have been involved in the accident.

TOO BEAUTIFUL TO DIE
Martin Carroll

There was a grave in the churchyard to prove Elizabeth Weston was dead. Alive, she presented a problem. Dead, she could be forgotten. Then, in the eighth year of her death she came back. She was beautiful, but she had to die.

IN COLD PURSUIT
Ursula Curtiss

In Mexico, Mary and her cousin Jenny each encounter strange men, but neither of them realises that one of these men is obsessed with revenge and murder. But which one?